2022

WORD WEAVERS

Edited By Allie Jones

First published in Great Britain in 2022 by:

Young Writers
Remus House
Coltsfoot Drive
Peterborough
PE2 9BF
Telephone: 01733 890066
Website: www.youngwriters.co.uk

Printed and bound in the UK by BookPrintingUK
Website: www.bookprintinguk.com
YB0522Q

FOREWORD

Welcome, Reader!

Are you ready to step into someone else's shoes and experience a new point of view?

For our latest competition *Twisted Tales*, we challenged secondary school students to write a story in just 100 words that shows us another side to the story. They could add a twist to an existing tale, show us a new perspective or simply write an original tale. They were given optional story starters and plot ideas for a spark of inspiration, and encouraged to consider the impact of narrative voice and theme.

The authors in this anthology have given us some unique new insights into tales we thought we knew, and written stories that are sure to surprise! The result is a thrilling and absorbing collection of stories written in a variety of styles, and it's a testament to the creativity of these young authors.

Here at Young Writers it's our aim to inspire the next generation and instill in them a love of creative writing, and what better way than to see their work in print? The imagination and skill within these pages are proof that we might just be achieving that aim! Congratulations to each of these fantastic authors.

CONTENTS

Aberdare Community School, Aberdare

Neve Paxton (11)   1
Joshua King (14)   2
Ffion Davies (12)   3
Ashlee Cumner (14)   4
Megan Stephens (12)   5
Lowan-Jay Davies (12)   6
Riley-Jay Johnson (12)   7
Leon Farinha (14)   8
Finley Blenkinsop-Clarke (12)   9
Joseph Matthews (12)   10
Jenna-Louise Gunter (14)   11
Lewis Nicholas (12)   12
Aaliyah-Marie Bevan (12)   13
Sophie Gullick (11)   14
Eve Williams (12)   15
Qasim Hameed (14)   16
Samuel Davies (12)   17
Marcus Longley (14)   18
Grace Evans (14)   19
Keira-Starr Hansen (14)   20
Elise Airey (14)   21
Harley Davies (12)   22
Kristian Paxford (12)   23
Jake Stone (14)   24
Lille-May Lloyd (12)   25
Paige Gamlin (14)   26
Ruby Davey (13)   27
Sophia Barnett (12)   28
Chloe Watson (11)   29
Riley Shellard (14)   30
Lara Leite (14)   31
Louisa Mears (12)   32
Phoebe Harris (14)   33
Lucas Harvey (12)   34
Kirsty Stevens (14)   35
Lewi Dutton (14)   36
Aimee Webb (14)   37
Lexi Pritchard (14)   38
Daniella Jones (12)   39
Logan Jones (12)   40
Imogen (12)   41
Lexi Morgan (14)   42
Brandon Jones (12)   43
Chloe Bryant (14)   44
Stacey Tshuma (12)   45
Harri Lagdon (14)   46
Carys jayne Jayne George (14)   47
Gwen Reddy (12)   48
Poppy Bricknell (12)   49
Dilan Mahmood (11)   50
William George Rowlands (14)   51

Greenford High School, Southall

Rooda Ahmed (13)   52

Helsby High School, Helsby

George Ferguson (13)   53
Rebecca Dodd (12)   54
Henry Jones (14)   55
Saffron Moorcroft (15)   56
Harry Webster (12)   57
Sophie Brennan (13)   58
Erin Price (14)   59
Max Hutton-Clarke (12)   60
Sophia Van Gordon (12)   61
Tillie Sherrington (13)   62
Max Cochrane (12)   63

Maisie Forster (12)	64	Zac Stanton (11)	102
Mischa Hendry (14)	65	Riley Milton (13)	103
Lola O'Brien (15)	66	Eva-Lilie Smith (12)	104
Izzy Brown (15)	67	Willow Stephenson (13)	105
Lewis Blake (12)	68	Niamh Roberts (13)	106
Isabelle Hartley (12)	69	Miles Bradbury-Webb (13)	107
Asa Joynson (12)	70	Mollie Lavers (12)	108
Nieve Dimelow (12)	71	Mason Vosper (12)	109
Philippe Lemmon (12)	72	Pixie Elliott (12)	110
Willow Walton (12)	73	Heidi Mudge (12)	111
Heidi Robertson (12)	74	Heidi Bassett (14)	112
Kyle Grant (15)	75	Jack Welsman (12)	113
Josh Cropper (13)	76	Tommy Lane (13)	114
Morgan Hughes (13)	77	Eddie Keaney (12)	115
Evie Maddock (12)	78	Toby Kent (11)	116
Luc Simpson (14)	79	Lewis Talmage (13)	117
Jake Thakur (12)	80	Sienna Bell (12)	118
Lilia Worthington (12)	81	Tyler King (13)	119
Rylee Thompson-Price (12)	82	Isla Ashford (13)	120
Scott Antrobus (12)	83	Olivia Smith (13)	121
Cole Matthews (12)	84	Jake Cox (13)	122
Oliver Cavanagh (12)	85	Isla Young (13)	123
Grace Lynch (12)	86	Maddox Healy (12)	124
Sophie Halsall-Cleworth (13)	87	Charlie Gibson (12)	125
Isla Seymour (12)	88	George Hillyer (13)	126
		Maya Chapple (12)	127

Penrice Academy, St Austell

		Lucas Mackney (12)	128
		Sam Dado (12)	129
James Bishop (14)	89	James Burdon (13)	130
Adriana Curtis (13)	90	Molly Howe (12)	131
Zlata Skokova (14)	91	Liam Talmage (13)	132
Tabitha Pinch (13)	92	April Howitt (13)	133
Megan Jeffreys (12)	93	Freya Edwards-Ede (12)	134
		Oliver Eastman (12)	135

Plympton Academy, Plympton

		Tayla Madavan (13)	136
		Reuben Lamude (12)	137
Katie Harvey (13)	94	Isabel Allen (13)	138
Josh Buckley (12)	95	Ruby Friend (13)	139
Logan Conlon (12)	96	Ethan Sterland (12)	140
Nathanael Wildgoose (12)	97	Lilia Abbott (13)	141
Jack Jones (13)	98	Mason Ebanks (12)	142
Megan Myles (13)	99	Dylan Fuller (12)	143
Lyra Docton (13)	100	Erin Shepherd (13)	144
Logan Findlay (12)	101		

Emily Scott-Davies (13)	145	Ruby Allen (12)	185
Zachary Bamford (13)	146	Eve Bateman (12)	186
Ellie Pritchard (12)	147	Nicole Luke (12)	187
Sophia Thrift (12)	148	Aiden Ridley (11)	188
Logan Kirk (12)	149	Amy Reeve (12)	189
Willow Aitchison (13)	150	Frankie Garraghan (12)	190
Will Ford (13)	151		
Faith Walsh (13)	152		

Westfield Academy, Yeovil

Grace Mitchell (13)	191

Jamie Boyes (12)	153
Rhys Slade (13)	154
Bethany Prowse (13)	155
George Adkins (11)	156
Charlie Matthews (13)	157
Elana Taylor (12)	158
Hayden Watters (13)	159
Harlee Mutch (12)	160
Oliver Ewing (13)	161
Harry Maloney (11)	162
Oliver Batten (12)	163
Joshua Pardoe (12)	164
Alex Piora (13)	165
Ava Mason (13)	166
Lizzy Griffiths (12)	167
Isabela Kingdom (13)	168
Elika Gallais-Worth (13)	169
Harvey Llewellyn (13)	170
Millie Webb (12)	171
Lucas Canning (12)	172
Owen Collings (13)	173
Kaleb Dolling (13)	174
Annabelle Staddon (12)	175
Emily Bennett (13)	176
Jack Simpson (12)	177
Jessica Richmond (13)	178
Nathan Annetts (13)	179

Wellfield Community School, Wingate

Holly Hesler (13)	180
Efa Hope Wilson (12)	181
Layla Richards (12)	182
Katie Colling (11)	183
Dexter Basford (12)	184

THE
STORIES

PETER'S TRUE STORY

Peter Pan is a kidnapper and nothing more. He takes kids and traps them in Neverland forever!

"I won't stop until all the kids in London are mine!" Peter yelled.

"You stop now!" a mysterious figure said to Peter.

"H-how?" Peter said, under his breath. The mysterious figure was Harry Hook, a boy he thought he'd captured who had escaped!

"I will end you!" Peter yelled.

They started fighting. *Clash! Bang!*

Hook fell into the water. But before he got back on land, a crocodile bit his hand off! "I will get you, Peter, mark my words! Some day, somehow..."

Neve Paxton (11)

Aberdare Community School, Aberdare

THE FLIGHT

As the flight attendant handed back my ticket, she slipped a small piece of paper between the folds. The handwriting was rushed. It read 'Rule 1 do not share this note. Rule 2 do not converse with them'. I chuckled, "Them, huh."
A man sat next to me. "How are you?"
Goosebumps ran down my arm. I remembered rule 1 and ignored him until a stewardess approached me.
"Is this man bothering you?"
I said, "Yes, he i-" I choked on my words, suddenly recalling rule 2.
Their heads snapped to me, grinning sinisterly, while blood fell from their eyes...

Joshua King (14)
Aberdare Community School, Aberdare

THE CUTLERY COUPLE

Ever wondered what happened to the cutlery couple? Where the delicate duo went? After the cat played the fiddle, the cow jumped and the dog barked, our dish and spoon had an exciting life.

"I've had enough of this rhyme!" exclaimed the spoon.

And with that, the dish and spoon left and didn't come back. They travelled to France, Fiji, the Philippines, America, Argentina and Aberdare. They travelled to China for the sights and smells and walked the Great Wall of China. However, the Chinese had never heard of talking silverware before and threw them off the Great Wall. *Crash!*

Ffion Davies (12)
Aberdare Community School, Aberdare

AVERTED DEATH

By famous Lady Macbeth's request, thirsty for power Macbeth left to kill his rightful king in cold blood. Meanwhile, the king was resting peacefully in his chambers unknowing of Macbeth's betraying sin he would commit. Macbeth entered, daggers in hand, preparing to commit the biggest act of treason known to man until Duncan woke, looking at Mabeth in pure shock. Macbeth froze in the process. Macbeth was caught, meaning he didn't kill Duncan but instead he lost his position of Thane of Cawdor but he and his wife were forgiven and the witches were blamed for messing with their minds.

Ashlee Cumner (14)
Aberdare Community School, Aberdare

THE MONSTER

As Frankenstein's monster awoke, he tried to express his gratitude of being brought to life but Frankenstein, his creator, seemed terrified of him. The monster was quite confused, as whenever he approached Frankenstein he would flee from him. This made the monster feel very lonely and isolated.

The monster ran away to start a new life and make friends. The monster wandered into the city and was nervous people would run away like the scientist. But, to his surprise, people loved him! They showed him around, invited him to eat and even visit their homes. He lived happily ever after.

Megan Stephens (12)
Aberdare Community School, Aberdare

THE BATTLE OF DEATH

It was a vicious fight between Spider-Man and Flash. They were fighting to the death. The Flash phased through a wall and punched Spider-Man out of nowhere. Spider-Man got up, shot webs and got him stuck to a wall and started punching him. The floor started shaking. There was thunder everywhere and a villain called Dormammu appeared who was trying to take over the world. The heroes rushed there. They teamed up and started fighting. Dormammu was strong, they couldn't beat him. They made one dangerous attack which killed one of them. They'd done it but Flash and Dormammu died.

Lowan-Jay Davies (12)
Aberdare Community School, Aberdare

HARRY POTTER

There was a person named Harry. When he was a child his parents were slaughtered by a wizard called Voldemort. It was an ordinary day until a white owl came and left Harry a letter inviting him to Hogwarts, but Harry's adoptive parents wouldn't let him go so the owl kept sending thousands of letters flooding Harry's house. Eventually, a wizard burst into his house called Hagrid and then Harry's parents let him go to Hogwarts. He made loads of friends and then a hat picked their class. It was Harry's turn. The hat picked Slytherin. Voldemort and Harry fought!

Riley-Jay Johnson (12)
Aberdare Community School, Aberdare

WHEN RATATOUILLE OBEYED HEALTH AND SAFETY LAWS

It was another day in Paris, Gusteau's was bustling with customers. It was cold when Linguini entered the kitchen, feeling the warmth and letting out a sigh of relief. Suddenly, he heard scuttling, followed by the sound of metal pots sliding around on their worktop. Investigating further, Linguini was shocked by what he saw, a rat seasoning a soup he was going to serve! He grabbed a broom, chasing it around the kitchen, trying to push it out. He gave up after a while and called an extermination company, who gladly accepted to take care of the restaurant's pest problem.

Leon Farinha (14)
Aberdare Community School, Aberdare

HUMPTY DUMPTY

This story begins when an average-sized egg is seen kicking his legs on the wall. Then after a while, the police come along and just look at the egg and then they ask the egg what his name is and why he's up there. Then the egg replies, "Humpty Dumpty and I actually don't know, sir." Then they say, "I think you should come down, buddy." After talking for quite a while, the egg nearly falls but then the police say, "Come down, buddy."
Then the police help Humpty Dumpty down and he says to the police, "Thank you."

Finley Blenkinsop-Clarke (12)
Aberdare Community School, Aberdare

IF I WAS IN HUMPTY DUMPTY

I would see Humpty Dumpty trying to go up to the wall. I would tell him, "Do not go up there."
"What, why?"
"Because you will fall," I said.
"Yeah, okay," Humpty Dumpty said in a sarcastic voice.
"DO NOT!" I shouted.
"Why?" asked Humpty Dumpty.
"Because you will fall and get hurt or die!"
"NO, I WON'T!"
So I went on the wall and fell on purpose so he did not want to go up on top of the wall because he did not want to as he might get hurt or die.

Joseph Matthews (12)
Aberdare Community School, Aberdare

HUNTED

Crack! Take another step you'll get chased, all he wants is fresh flesh. The clown chases little kids down the street. He can almost smell his prey from miles away. There are helicopters and armed police everywhere looking for him. He runs into the dark. Don't go there. You'd better be careful if you want to survive; there's more than one. He'll almost drag you down into the darkest parts and then eat off of you. He'll make a child scream. It gets so loud and then almost silent. He's being hunted down. You could call it... hunted.

Jenna-Louise Gunter (14)
Aberdare Community School, Aberdare

GOLDILOCKS

She ate the porridge. They came back. She apologised but in a rage, the daddy bear ate her after she'd trashed the place.

Her father, who was a hunter, asked, "Where is my daughter?"

The mother replied, "She hasn't returned yet."

The father went out with a search party. They found the bear cottage and the daddy bear answered the door. They shot and he fell. The mother bear hid the baby bear while she checked it out. She found the father holding Goldilocks. She was shot dead and the baby bear was left alone for a while.

Lewis Nicholas (12)
Aberdare Community School, Aberdare

HANSEL AND GRETEL

There were two kids, Hansel and Gretel. One day their father took them hunting for animals and wood for fires. Their father mysteriously decided to disappear and leave them alone in the woods. Lost and confused, they looked for help. They came across a lonely colourful cottage, somehow made of candy. They took a bite of the delicious pleasure. They knocked the door three loud times. The door opened with a creak. A witch appeared from the dark. She dragged the children inside and tried to hurt them. They decided to burn the witch, but it didn't go to plan...

Aaliyah-Marie Bevan (12)

Aberdare Community School, Aberdare

GOLDILOCKS

She finds herself in a forest. In the distance, she sees a cabin. She builds up her courage to go see what it's about. As she walks in, a strong smell floods the room. She goes to where the smell's coming from: three bowls of porridge sit in front of her. She tries one. "Too cold!" she says. She tries another. "It's too hot," she says. As she tries another she says, "Just right!" She starts to head upstairs. She walks into the room. A huge shadow appears. A loud scream floods the forest and she isn't seen again.

Sophie Gullick (11)
Aberdare Community School, Aberdare

MR SCISSOR HANDS

Once, a young girl came across an old and scrappy house. She went strawberry picking in a nearby bush.
"Hello girl," someone shouted. The girl was confused.
The girl went inside and saw a long, shadowy figure with scissor hands appear. He slayed everyone who trespassed. But since she was so young, he couldn't do it.
He looked after her day after day, until one night he snapped. He hung her next to his bed and cried on her blood every night. He stabbed everyone who trespassed in his house. Nobody has heard about him since.

Eve Williams (12)
Aberdare Community School, Aberdare

MARVELLOUS MACBETH

The news came out Duncan had died, but not killed, he naturally died. Macbeth was devastated. However, he was now king of Scotland. Lady Macbeth was also very sad deep down.

The first thing Macbeth did was remove taxes and lower gas prices. Everyone liked him as king they thought he was better than Duncan. To show how much Macbeth cared for the country he gave the people of Scotland new homes to stay. Everyone loved the new houses.

Macbeth and Lady Macbeth had a baby boy and named him Macbeth II. Macbeth II went on to rule Scotland later.

Qasim Hameed (14)
Aberdare Community School, Aberdare

BAD WOLF'S BAD LIFE

This story begins with a bad wolf, his three cubs and wife. These wolves haven't eaten in days. They live under a tree, are struggling to pay rent and the wife is an alcoholic and has started to eat mushrooms just to cure their thirst for meat. The wolves' only chance to get food is the three pigs that moved a few blocks away. He went to the brick house and said, "Come out!"

The pigs said, "No!"

He tried to break in but it didn't come down. He started sobbing for dear life and they all died of starvation.

Samuel Davies (12)

Aberdare Community School, Aberdare

THE TRUTH BEHIND GENERAL GRIEVOUS

General Grievous wasn't always the Jedi-killing war machine everyone knows, he had a much different life before joining the Dark Side. He was originally a Kaleesh male warlord who went by the name Qymaen Jai Sheelal. His life started the downward spiral after he lost the love of his life and knew he had to mourn her forever. He eventually crashed his space shuttle and was mortally wounded and the only way to save him was to reconstruct his body. Grievous then went on to kill more as a separatist leader and went on to rule the galaxy.

Marcus Longley (14)
Aberdare Community School, Aberdare

WILLY WONKA'S 'CHOCOLATE' FACTORY

The plan was in motion, the five children had arrived at the chocolate oak-stained door. A signature snide smirk was sprawled across Mr Wonka's face. He lifted his arm and adjusted his hat, then lifted another and guided the children inside. Little did they know they would never walk out.
The first to go was the giant Mr Gloop, sucked into a tube and tangled and twisted through the pipes until he was like his name - a gloop. Then he was taken to the room and transformed into the very thing he enjoyed most... a bar of chocolate.

Grace Evans (14)
Aberdare Community School, Aberdare

PERCY'S BETRAYAL

Percy was standing close to Luke, blade in hand. He had attempted to stop Luke multiple times, but it wasn't working. He tried again but then he thought of something. What had the gods ever done for him? Hell, they voted to kill him once. He called for Kronos and asked if he was ready. Annabeth gasped as her face turned to pure shock when she realised he was betraying her. Her face turned from shock to dread as he said, "Destroy Olympus and the gods," and handed him his weapon. He shrugged and turned to Annabeth, smiling.

Keira-Starr Hansen (14)

Aberdare Community School, Aberdare

MACBETH

Banquo and Duncan decide to team up against Macbeth himself, they feel as though Macbeth and Lady Macbeth have a plan. Duncan sets Banquo up to spy on Macbeth and Lady Macbeth to see what they're up to. Lady Macbeth is telling Macbeth how he should commit regicide but he doesn't want to follow her plan. Lady Macbeth comes for Macbeth saying he needs to be more manly, after Banquo listens he goes to see Macbeth later on in the day. Duncan and Banquo do not like Lady Macbeth and they plan to kill her. Macbeth teams up with them.

Elise Airey (14)
Aberdare Community School, Aberdare

MINIONS' BETRAYAL

Gru had planned to steal the moon again. Last time it didn't go as planned. He recreated the shrink ray so the object didn't go back to its regular shape. He then told the Minions about his evil plan. The Minions didn't like the plan so they decided to betray him. Bob had a very evil idea. He murdered Gru and told everyone his idea. He wanted to rescue Vector from the moon. They all agreed and decided to build a rocket. Soon it was complete, they went to save Vector. They rescued him and went to claim Gru's house.

Harley Davies (12)
Aberdare Community School, Aberdare

NO ROOM ON THE BROOM

There once was a witch named Emily. When she was young she saw many animals in desperation and in need. Emily wanted to help those in need, so built a broom and made loads of room. What Emily didn't know was there wasn't enough room. She tried to fit all the animals on the broom but there wasn't enough room. She tried adding more but then a catastrophe happened. She tried fitting a frog and the frog was a little big and pushed her off... She lost her broom and the animals left her in the middle of nowhere alone...

Kristian Paxford (12)
Aberdare Community School, Aberdare

THE PIG INVASION

There was a colony of wolves, a very bad colony of wolves. We, the Pigs, went exploring and found land that was only inhabited by very rude wolves. We went over to find land to live on but they just kept pestering us saying, "We welcome you to our land." How is it their land?
So as all normal people, we got rid of them in any way possible. Well, we thought we kille-, I mean got rid of them. Now there was one wolf that just went everywhere destroying our houses.
Then we found him and executed him publicly.

Jake Stone (14)
Aberdare Community School, Aberdare

THE JEALOUS FORK

One day, there was a fork, a spoon and a dish. It was a hot summer's day and the dish and spoon sprinted into the distance together. The fork was jealous of their relationship, but little did she know they were dating.

Years later, the spoon and dish were living their best life, having kids and living together, but the fork wasn't happy and wanted revenge. She set up lots of plans to break the spoon and dish up. One plan worked and now the fork and dish are living their best lives while the spoon is all alone.

Lille-May Lloyd (12)

Aberdare Community School, Aberdare

BETWEEN HEAVEN AND HELL

A disappointed God stood before me, I then awoke in Hell. My job was to kill others how I pleased. I killed thousands of criminals for their crimes, whether it be natural causes or murder. It depended on the severity of their crimes. I thought I'd be given a second chance at life this way, but I should've never trusted a sinner. Nobody knew the truth about me. I wasn't a villain, that man deserved to be struck down by my blade. Now I'm stuck here for all of eternity, regretting all the things I've done.

Paige Gamlin (14)
Aberdare Community School, Aberdare

BUCKY BARNES WANTS REVENGE

The same moment plays in his head. The same nightmare that keeps him awake. James Buchanan Barnes is his name. Bucky is what he's called. He wakes up in a cold sweat, in fear. The nightmares get worse every time he tries to sleep. He wants to forget the things he's done and what he's been through. Hydra, the war, the people he's killed. He can't take it back. But he wants to. He nearly murdered his best friend while under the control of Hydra. They made Bucky suffer, he wants revenge. He will get it...

Ruby Davey (13)
Aberdare Community School, Aberdare

THE TWISTED MERMAID

One salty day under the sea, Ariel went to Ursula for help. She wanted legs. So, she asked the sea witch for legs. Although she got her legs, her voice was completely gone. She swam up on shore to find her fiancé, but saw him marrying Ursula. She was furious. She tried to scream but nothing came out. So she ran and pounced on him. She knocked him to the floor and murdered him. Shocked by her actions, she ran. She cried and cried until the police took her away. She was then given a life sentence.
Ursula cried.

Sophia Barnett (12)
Aberdare Community School, Aberdare

THE BIG BAD WOLF

Once upon a time, a wolf lived in the forest. The wolf was a single father with three kids. No food was in the forest anymore, they were all hungry. One day the wolf went hunting again and there was a girl wearing a red hood. She was going to her grandmother's. The wolf's plan was to get to the grandmother's before her and pretend to be her grandmother and eat them both. So the wolf ran to the house, killed the grandmother dressed in her clothes and Little Red Riding Hood walked in and then it all happened...

Chloe Watson (11)
Aberdare Community School, Aberdare

SPIDER-MAN BUT HIS POWERS ARE LIMITED

This story's about Peter Parker, a student who spends most of their time in either school or The Daily Bugle. Until one day, while taking photos for his school, he was bitten by a not-so-radioactive spider. He found out that he could wall climb using just his hands, but he could only climb if he kept moving because he would start to slip. Peter went home later that day and found out his uncle was shot by a mugger. He found out where this mugger was and tried to stop him but he was robbed and was never seen again.

Riley Shellard (14)
Aberdare Community School, Aberdare

MEDUSA

As Medusa walks past hundreds of statues of men who have come to slay her, she weeps in sorrow, knowing she can never look someone in the eyes ever again. Suddenly, she hears a statue fall. Medusa turns around and prepares herself to see another blindfolded man ready to attack. Instead she sees a man shaking, covering his eyes and holding out a pair of sunglasses. She takes them and steps back. As she puts them on she can see the man has stopped covering his eyes. She just stares into his eyes and nothing happens...

Lara Leite (14)
Aberdare Community School, Aberdare

ROMEO AND JULIET

I'm not proud of what I've done. But it had to happen. Juliet was too attached to Romeo. It was never going to work between them anyway. I created a plan to get Romeo away from my daughter forever. The plan was brilliant and clever, but they messed it up. First, I slipped Romeo a note, telling him that Juliet was dead. When he rushed to her room while she was asleep, I stabbed him and quietly walked away. I didn't expect her to kill herself over some arrogant boy. She wasn't supposed to act that way!

Louisa Mears (12)
Aberdare Community School, Aberdare

EVIL QUEEN'S REASONS

Before the death of the king, I felt invisible. I was always alone and whenever the king spoke it was about how radiant Snow White or her mother was. I never wanted to replace her, but to feel loved. After the king's death I became queen. For the first time in a long time I felt seen. Snow White was still a reminder of how insecure and invisible the king made me feel. So I sent men to kill her and stop my suffering. Everybody says I'm the villain, but maybe the only difference is who is telling the story?

Phoebe Harris (14)
Aberdare Community School, Aberdare

THE GINGERBREAD WAR

Once upon a time, there was a German baker who created a super weapon known as Gingee (me). One day I'd enough of the baker and escaped to join Britain in WWII. During the battle of France, I realised there were other gingerbread men. Then a gingerbread army as big as a whale attacked me. After a major defeat in France, I quickly went back out to fight. I used my minigun to mow down the enemy. I murdered many and in an attempt to save my friends, I started punching them until we all lay lifeless on the floor.

Lucas Harvey (12)
Aberdare Community School, Aberdare

MACDUFF'S STORY

Before Macbeth became king, he was a worthy man, a man that everybody respected. But something changed in him, something turned him into a violent monster. He destroyed my life by taking the ones I loved the most and taking my home away from me. I was destroyed by the news as one would be. So when the sons of Duncan declared war on Macbeth I had to join the fight. When I saw Macbeth on the battlefield, I felt all the anger build up inside of me. After killing Macbeth I thought I'd be happy but I'm empty.

Kirsty Stevens (14)
Aberdare Community School, Aberdare

RON'S JEALOUSY

It all started when my mum enrolled me into Hogwarts School for Witchcraft and Wizardry. I came across this strange boy who I recognised and then it hit me, it was Harry Potter. I sat next to him on the train, giving him a wide smile.

When we arrived at Hogwarts I was amazed by the scenery. I sat on the Sorting Hat chair and was happy as I was in Gryffindor, but Harry got a louder and longer applause. I felt my blood boil. He was getting all the attention about his scar. The jealousy flared up inside me...

Lewi Dutton (14)
Aberdare Community School, Aberdare

TWISTED PAN

I have to tell you a story about Peter Pan.

Peter lives in a place called Neverland, it's covered in rough trees and beautiful clear waters. However, Peter didn't always live here, he was once a boy and one year he made a wish and it came true. He wished for everlasting life and to live somewhere no adults could tell him what to do. But there was something missing, he was lonely. He longed for a friend. A portal had grown. He used it and before I knew it I was trapped with him. I can't leave.

Aimee Webb (14)
Aberdare Community School, Aberdare

THE WOLF AND PIGS AT WAR

Many moons ago, there was a village called Aberdare. In Aberdare the pigs lived and Mountain Ash was where the wolves lived. The pigs always hated the wolves for no reason. One day they made up a plan to destroy the wolves. The pigs stuck to the plan and the pigs set up their army and went on a train to Mountain Ash.

When the pigs came off the train, the pigs immediately started to declare war. The wolves had no clue what the pigs were doing. The pigs thought they killed every wolf but they were wrong.

Lexi Pritchard (14)

Aberdare Community School, Aberdare

BEAUTY AND THE BEAST

I found myself panicked. A bright light came down; the flower the Beast had had fallen apart. I tried to save him but before I knew it, he wasn't breathing. He was gone... My prince was no longer.

After that, Gaston forced me to marry him. Not only that, I had to live in the castle that he had lived in. The house was renovated and all the old items that moved didn't; the spark that the castle had was lost... I am now 48 and I still can't get over what happened many years ago. I miss him.

Daniella Jones (12)
Aberdare Community School, Aberdare

BEAR HUNT

Welcome to the modern day but now we are not in the modern day. We are now in the day before yesterday but 6 million years before then. This is also the first time man and family have hunted a bear also known as the first Bear Hunt. When then the bear had eaten the two kids, the survivors proceeded to kill the bear and freed the two kids that had not been digested yet. The family were hungry so they ate the bear but the bear's skeleton came back to life. Then the family lived until they passed away.

Logan Jones (12)
Aberdare Community School, Aberdare

THE MYSTERIOUS MATILDA

It was one ordinary day for three-year-old Matilda, her mother was going to work in a cafe and her father had to go to build some houses. Matilda's brother had to look after her. When she was four, she went to school. She loved to read. She was very smart but her teacher didn't like it. The teacher said to the head that she wanted Matilda in a different class but she said no. The next day the head teacher took Matilda home with her and asked if she was okay to go up a class. Matilda said yes...

Imogen (12)
Aberdare Community School, Aberdare

MACBETH

It was a normal day until Macbeth came home and told me he wanted to kill the king. I was very happy about it because I wanted to be the queen. Later on in the day, Macbeth told me he wasn't sure about his decision. I was very annoyed because I wanted to be queen and I wanted all the power, so I decided to kill Macbeth but that made things worse. That night, me and Macbeth were supposed to be going to dinner with the king but Macbeth was dead. I didn't know what to do. I regretted everything.

Lexi Morgan (14)
Aberdare Community School, Aberdare

THE TEENS TRAVEL INTO THE WOODS

There were three teens on a road trip, Brandon, Jordan and Ella. They were all 17. They were travelling on a road through the woods. They got scared and pulled over but realised the car had no petrol. So they went into the woods because they heard a strange noise. They were walking for about thirty minutes until they found a figure with bright red eyes. Then they saw it was eating a deer so they ran and were saved because someone came with a can of petrol. They lived happily ever after.

Brandon Jones (12)

Aberdare Community School, Aberdare

FOREVER SLEEPING BEAUTY

The plan is in motion. Princess Aurora, the most beautiful girl in the village, is destined to be mine by the end of the night. She will be mine forever. The love of my life. I have designed a perfect plan to make her mine. She will have no choice but to accept it. I am Prince Phillip and I have planned to make all of her problems disappear. By the end of the night her finger will be pricked, her food poisoned and a spell cast upon her. She will fall into a dreamless sleep never to wake.

Chloe Bryant (14)
Aberdare Community School, Aberdare

NEVER JUDGE A BOOK BY ITS COVER

Nobody knew the truth about me. My name's Kage, people thought I was a bad person, but deep down I was a good person. People called me names, I got kicked out of places. One day, I went for a walk in the park. I saw a girl that had the same problem as me until one day we saved a boy from falling from a tree. We tried to make friends and from that day people were good to us and they learned never to judge people for how they look, but from their hearts.
That is my story.

Stacey Tshuma (12)
Aberdare Community School, Aberdare

HUMPTY DUMPTY

Humpty Dumpty sat on a wall. Humpty Dumpty had a great fall; except he didn't crack or he didn't break. This is what really happened:
I just came back from the bakery, with a nice piece of pie. A long walk home made me tired, I had to stop or I felt I'd die.
I stopped at the bridge, my legs weak, and I really needed a bite to eat. I sat up on the side of the wall. I thought I better start on my pie.
I leaned back a bit too far and almost fell off the side!

Harri Lagdon (14)
Aberdare Community School, Aberdare

FEAR

I found myself on my hands and knees, mud in my hands, frightened, confused. As I looked up I saw a shovel. Where was I? I was frightened, I felt like I was paralysed. I was in a graveyard, but how did I get here? I slowly got up, freezing cold, and walked close to the grave that was dug up. It was a tunnel. Still in fear, the only thing I could do was walk into the dark tunnel, so I did. Suddenly, I heard footsteps running towards me from the darkness. I felt a lump in my throat...

Carys jayne Jayne George (14)

Aberdare Community School, Aberdare

THE CRAZY KIDNAPPING

I woke up as tired as ever, then suddenly woke up completely, with a startle. I was in the back of a van with my brothers, Stuart and Kevin. They were awake and panicking too! Then it came to a stop and we realised we were going all over the place. We looked through the blurred glass and we saw a tall figure. When it got closer, we realised they had red hair! It was Lucy! We were relieved so we screamed her name but she started laughing at us... But Gru came to the rescue!

Gwen Reddy (12)
Aberdare Community School, Aberdare

PETER AND THE NEVERLAND

Once upon a time, Peter took a trip down memory lane... to Neverland. He needed to beat his battle with Walter Hook! Little did he know, this time he was going to lose. Peter now returned to Walter's ship to see a big army. Peter was losing this battle badly and was getting very hurt. They finished the battle and Peter was badly hurt. Walter got his revenge by tying Peter to the sail and leaving him in the heat to die of heatstroke.

Poppy Bricknell (12)
Aberdare Community School, Aberdare

TARGETING HUMPTY

The king was hungry and wanted to eat eggs, but the only egg was Humpty-Dumpty. The king wanted to kill him without losing his reputation. He found out Humpty loved sitting on a brick wall, so he made it wobbly. After a while, Humpty kept on falling until he got badly injured so the king did it again and Humpty fell again and died.
When the news died down, the king took the body to the palace and ate him and nobody ever knew!

Dilan Mahmood (11)
Aberdare Community School, Aberdare

THE DREAM OF WAR

I woke up, all around me was the sound of bombs going off and gunshots from men. I got up and saw I had been dragged out of my own home to be taken to the war. I was face-to-face with one of my biggest fears - death. I started to panic but I have to tell you, I was ready. I got up from the makeshift bed I had slept in, got my gun and got to work. After a while, I was shot, all went black...
Then I woke up. All was normal.

William George Rowlands (14)

Aberdare Community School, Aberdare

BLOODLUST

Bathed in the moonlight, her gleaming golden dress flew in the wind, creating an illusion of a newborn flame roaring for destruction. Her silhouette skipped into the depths of the emerald forest, a sign decorated with blood lay neglected on the floor. Abruptly, a hair-raising shriek escaped the treacherous trap. Hesitantly venturing to investigate, she felt a crunch beneath her. It was a human heart. Flashing gold, her eyes held a ravenous stare - as if she was slowly losing a battle between her desires and needs. Her hands tore it apart. Not enough. She needed more. A human feast.

Rooda Ahmed (13)
Greenford High School, Southall

HOW I SAVED JURASSIC PARK

Crack! He burst open the door and called my name, "George! Come with me!" I followed him. Outside there was a helicopter with 'Dinosaur Capture Team' written on the side waiting for us. We hopped in and started flying somewhere. We flew for a while until I noticed we were at Jurassic Park, they needed my help capturing dinosaurs. The ones that had escaped were quite dangerous, like the T-rex and the spinosaurus. There was one dinosaur left to capture and Owen let me tranquilise it.

After that day, I was known as the person who helped save Jurassic Park.

George Ferguson (13)

Helsby High School, Helsby

ONE BIG MISTAKE...

I wasn't the 'perfect princess', we all make mistakes, but my one might have cost her her life.

Trapped in my tower, vulnerable, lonely, scared, I sobbed as I glared at my surroundings. Separated from the rest, I couldn't live this life anymore. I needed to flee immediately. After difficulty making it down the tower, I agreed to meet some of my friends who wanted to help me. I glanced and saw my evil mother behind me.

"Don't you dare run away from me!" she roared.

My friends were horrified. One of them didn't make it out alive...

Rebecca Dodd (12)

Helsby High School, Helsby

IKARI

Filtered image through inky strands, the stones she rested on cold and unfeeling. She leant over, strangely drawn. A calling into the abyss. Bleached skin gleamed, unfamiliar in the sunlight as ebony hair trailed and flawed vision struggled to see him. Brick raised, clenched, a gap in memory cut short by waking moments, struggling against a sickening sludge that seemed to swallow her into the maw of the well. An odious glance caught the last glimpse of light before it was shut off. Alne, scared in the darkness, undying hatred forever marred the world; a scar never to be healed.

Henry Jones (14)
Helsby High School, Helsby

TANGLED IN LOVE

Merciless eyes pierced with curiosity as they adventured up and down my face. One hand caressed the delicate cheek, the other came over my head, carefully running through the luminous streaks of blonde in my hair, reassuring the lost strands into place. My eyes fluttered with passion as they rose to meet his when malice washed over his expression. Drawing a blade from his pocket, murderously ripping through my hair and penetrating my vulnerable heart. Vacantly, he watched as the dark, rippling red pooled beneath me and the anchor of mankind left me like crows from a fallen oak.

Saffron Moorcroft (15)
Helsby High School, Helsby

THE JUNGLE MUMBLE

Once upon a time, a tiger called Shere Khan was found by a big friendly bear named Baloo. "Don't worry, little guy," Baloo said to him. He was very scared.
As he grew up Baloo sang a song called 'Bear Necessities' to him. He was like a dad to him.
Suddenly, an arrow flew right past Shere Khan's neck.
"Run, Shere Khan, run!"
It was a man, he had a bow. Baloo and Shere Khan hid with the monkeys. They helped attack the man, he was called Mowgli. He finally learned his lesson.
Suddenly, they heard a "Sssss!"

Harry Webster (12)
Helsby High School, Helsby

THE BEAST

A shrill sound came echoing along the winding forest as Belle sprinted for her life, Lumiere by her side. The Beast was following them with every ounce of fury he had left in him. *"No one escapes me!"* he roared, pouncing forward with a gut-wrenching grin etched on his face. Belle and Lumiere rapidly weaved through the trees, memories of that dilapidated cell haunting them. She halted in a trance of thoughts. The Beast rose up above her, breaking the silence. Lumiere fell to the ground, begging for mercy as Belle accepted her horrific but certain fate...

Sophie Brennan (13)
Helsby High School, Helsby

ALICE IN HELL

Alice ran, her blood cold with fear. She could hear the cards catching up. The shrieking of the queen rang in her ears. "Off with her head!" the cards chanted. Alice suddenly tripped on a vine and fell hard to the ground. She had to keep going before the once colourful and beautifully insane world engulfed her in darkness and death.

Alice went to get up but found the vine twisting tightly around her ankles. She was trapped. Suddenly, a pair of ice-cold blue eyes stared at her in the darkness. The face grinned maliciously. "You belong to me!"

Erin Price (14)
Helsby High School, Helsby

A STRANGE CHANGE

I woke up in my bed, wearing my pyjamas. Everything was different. Large flying dinosaurs ruled the skies and others roamed the dense grassland. My eyes glistened with happiness, but I had to seek shelter. If I didn't I wouldn't live much longer.

As I was finding camp, large herds of dinosaurs stomped past me, but they weren't trying to kill me. Smoke wafted towards me and volcanic rocks flew towards me. Could this be?

I ran with all my might and fell into a large hole. I was stuck. After a few minutes, lava began reaching the hole...

Max Hutton-Clarke (12)

Helsby High School, Helsby

BEAUTY IN DISTRESS

The stone floor was rigid against my pale hands. A faint voice was heard outside the walls. I scurried over until I hit the barrier between us. I screamed but nothing was heard. They were talking to someone, but no one responded. Suddenly, a roar echoed through the cave. Was it to me or not? I couldn't tell. It was outside because the clashing of swords and screams could be heard. A flame suddenly swarmed around me when the sounds disappeared. My breathing hitched. The last thing I remember was the solid floor, my panting and my blurry eyesight.

Sophia Van Gordon (12)
Helsby High School, Helsby

MY SISTER AND THE SECRET

I feel bad for Cinderella, I always have, but if your mother was like mine you'd stay quiet too. I would help her with chores, save her food and make sure she had something to wear. However, I don't think many people know my story. I don't have a happy ending or a happy beginning. But I'm okay with that.

I now work in my stepsister's castle. I wouldn't consider myself a nice person, I have done too much. I'm not pretty or smart or kind like Cinderella. The thing that really makes me a bad person is my secret...

Tillie Sherrington (13)
Helsby High School, Helsby

THE TRUE STORY OF CAPTAIN HOOK

Captain Hook was a very downcast and depressed pirate because a kid called Peter Pan was picking on him. Captain Hook was disabled as he had no arm because a crocodile had bitten it off. But Captain Hook was irritated and indignant because these brats were coming every day and being very disrespectful. Captain Hook was annoyed because the kids were coming to harass him every day for weeks and months and years. Poor Captain Hook was in despair, he could not sleep at night. He tossed and turned and decided to hatch a cunning plan for revenge...

Max Cochrane (12)
Helsby High School, Helsby

ME AND MY CHILDHOOD

Nobody knew the truth about me. Everyone thinks that I'm the happy girl from the Wizard of Oz, Dorothy. Yeah, that's me. My life's been a roller coaster, living with five brothers and four sisters. Our parents find it hard to handle. I've never really had a happy childhood that most other kids do. But all that changed when I met a tin man, a lion and a scarecrow. I love them all like they're my second family. We've had so many exciting adventures together and they've helped me so and changed my life for the better.

Maisie Forster (12)
Helsby High School, Helsby

IF PETER PAN CAME BACK FOR WENDY

It almost felt like déjà vu, but this time I didn't feel the thrill of returning back to London in 2022. Fifty years ago it was fun, soaring over the sky full of stars. It was different now though. The skies that used to be the home of the stars had turned into a blanket of black smoke and the streets were cramped like sardines in a tin.

As I finally returned to where the Darling home once was, I glanced down at the building to see nothing but office blocks. My heart sank. She wasn't there. Wendy was gone.

Mischa Hendry (14)

Helsby High School, Helsby

ADAM'S FIRST WIFE

I'm on the warpath. Adam's first wife, the one you don't hear about. The one created before Eve was formed from his rib. The one who didn't submit, who wouldn't bend over backwards to his every wish. The one cast down to Hell for being powerful. Avenged as one of the four queens of Hell. Reborn as royalty. I'm almost there, from the speed of the highway to Hell to the eternal marching of the stairway to Heaven. Eve is his new wife, submissive and weak, formed from his rib. I am their superior. I am royalty.

Lola O'Brien (15)
Helsby High School, Helsby

JACK AND JILL - WHAT REALLY HAPPENED

No one but me knows what really happened that day. It was a warm spring day. Birds were chirping, flowers blooming. Over in the distance, two young people seemed to be rowing. They had been sent to collect a pail of water. They continued up the hill still rowing. Jill seemed very aggravated, with her mood only getting worse. Two minutes went by; no change in her mood. All of a sudden, Jill took the pail she was using to collect the water and she smashed Jack over the head, causing him to instantly die a bloody death.

Izzy Brown (15)

Helsby High School, Helsby

VOLDEMORT: ORIGINS

It was horrible, I was being bullied every day until this old man came to my orphanage. We talked about my abilities, he said there were more people like me at a school called Hogwarts.

On the day I went to the school, we were called up and I had a hat placed on my head and it told us our houses. Gryffindor, Hufflepuff, Ravenclaw or Slytherin. I was put in Slytherin, that's what I wanted. I'd heard that was the house for ambitious and courageous people. I felt like I could rule the world when I was older...

Lewis Blake (12)
Helsby High School, Helsby

ROMEO AND JULIET TWIST

Juliet and Romeo were madly in love. Romeo had been banned from Verona. Juliet made a plan. She took a sleeping potion and sent a letter to Romeo so he would come rushing to her. Then she would wake up in time. But Romeo didn't get the letter. His friend told him what happened and he went to Verona with a bottle of poison so he could be with Juliet.

Romeo got there and was about to drink the poison but Lady Juliet woke up. They ran away together so there would be no trouble at home and lived happily.

Isabelle Hartley (12)

Helsby High School, Helsby

HISTORY'S MOST IRONIC EVENT

It was late at night in the 1600s and the great Guy Fawkes was about to explode Parliament and finally be free. He had previously stored thousands of tonnes of gunpowder under Parliament and in a few minutes he was going blow it all up. So he lit a match and lit a trail of gunpowder and - *kaboom!* He had successfully blown up Parliament. But... he got killed in the explosion and never got to experience the free will we have today.
So if you try to do the same, leave Parliament before blowing it up!

Asa Joynson (12)

Helsby High School, Helsby

GOLDILOCKS' WAY OF SEEING THINGS

When I entered the bears' house, I didn't mean to mess anything up. I'd been out for days, so when I saw the open door, I went in. I saw the steaming porridge and tried it all. I thought it was a holiday house.

Later, when the bears arrived, I almost cried because Baby Bear was in tears. I didn't know what to do. So when they kicked me out, I understood why. I then went to buy them more porridge, new chairs and new beds. But when I got there they had gone, so I left a 'sorry' note.

Nieve Dimelow (12)

Helsby High School, Helsby

A WEREWOLF'S POINT OF VIEW

I wasn't supposed to be like this, they forced me to experiment on them. I had a family, until I was forced to go on the run. They'll never stop hunting for me for what I did. I was in a top-secret science experiment where we were experimenting on hyper animals with special abilities. I was doing work on a wolf when suddenly it bit me. When I got home I changed. I had a sudden need for human flesh, so I went to a village and that's where I did the horrible deed. And now they're hunting me...

Philippe Lemmon (12)
Helsby High School, Helsby

WOMEN'S RIGHTS

Our banner states 'Our bodies our choice' in big colourful writing for the parade tomorrow; my best friend Gemma has prepared. Last night it was announced that the Supreme Court in America is trying to ban abortions and that you could get 15 years in jail if you have one. Gemma is a young girl who is angered by this news, just like almost all women in America at the moment. And even though I am a man, I will stand up for women's rights.

That's all from me tonight. John Adams.

Willow Walton (12)

Helsby High School, Helsby

MY SCAR

My brother and I played together frequently. Once, we were playing and my brother scratched me for no reason. I ran to our father. Mufasa lied and said, "He tried to push me off a cliff!" Father was furious. He told me I could never be king because kings aren't murderers. I ran away. Father said I must live in a cave me and Mufasa made earlier and that I could never go back. My kingdom was Mufasa's. Tears and blood mixed when rolling down my face. And that is how I became Scar!

Heidi Robertson (12)

Helsby High School, Helsby

HANSEL AND GRETEL

The children were excited to find such a bright house in the forest. They surged forward, ignoring the signposts telling them to steer clear, and headed straight for the cotton candy windows. I saw it all, they fell into the trap as easily as I can grow a new wart. I opened the door slowly so I didn't spook them. I said hello and pulled out an AK-47 and shot them multiple times. I turned them into swiss cheese. I was wondering what I would have for tea, so skinned them like fish. Sorted.

Kyle Grant (15)
Helsby High School, Helsby

THE BEAST'S BALL

Once upon a time, there was a young man with a curse. He lived as a monster, a beast; he longed to be normal. The Beast heard of a ball where all could visit. This was his chance, however, it couldn't have gone worse. His monster senses kicked in and he killed everyone in sight. Even that wasn't enough as he went out hungry for more, and killed the much-loved Beauty. On the inside, he whimpered, but on the outside he was on the run. The guards were called and the Beast raced out...

Josh Cropper (13)
Helsby High School, Helsby

ENTER SANDMAN

As he, she, it, came into my room, I felt like I knew exactly what was coming my way. It seemed like my fate had finally been sealed. It came up to me and touched me with its heated fingers and I felt a massive rush of adrenaline in my body. As it finally came to an end, something felt off. I was not in my comforting room. No, I was in boiling surroundings with strange creatures who looked like guards. Then suddenly, I knew where I was. It was so obvious. I was trapped... in Hell.

Morgan Hughes (13)
Helsby High School, Helsby

THE REAL DR FACILIER

Before I became Dr Facilier, and became a voodoo magic legend, I was an alright person. You see what happened was when I was a young boy I broke into the real Dr Facilier's voodoo hut. Let's just say, he wasn't happy about it. He said he would read my fortune, but what I didn't know was in return he passed on the curse so he was free. Our parents always warned us to stay away but now I really knew why. I have to protect this necklace at all costs to keep my power.

Evie Maddock (12)
Helsby High School, Helsby

SHERE KHAN'S STORY

Nobody knows what really happened that night, but I will spill the truth. I'm Shere Khan, the king of the jungle and this is my story. I used to be weak and slow but when both of my parents died in an elephant stampede, I grew stronger and stronger until I was the strongest ever. Then one night I got burnt by fire and then a human came along and challenged me as the king of the jungle. I wanted to speak but he tried to burn me like the last human. I was scared so I ran away!

Luc Simpson (14)
Helsby High School, Helsby

THE INFECTED

My story starts while my parents were on honeymoon. I was home alone. My friend Joseph had turned quite strange. I'd never seen him like it before.

I heard banging on my window and I was confused. Who or what was it? They broke through so I quickly jumped out of the window - I didn't care how high it was. I looked back and saw my friend along with many other infected people. I freaked out. I ran away as fast as I could. I knew I was never going back there again.

Jake Thakur (12)
Helsby High School, Helsby

MY TRUE INTENTIONS

I'm Maleficent and nobody knows the truth about me. What people don't know is that I can see the future and when babies are born. When I saw Aurora, I had to put that spell on her, it was the only thing I could do. I saw on her 16th birthday, her true love would kill Aurora for the land. So I thought once I killed him I could wake her up from her sleep. So I had to scare the royals that only true love's kiss could wake her up so I could kill him and save Aurora.

Lilia Worthington (12)

Helsby High School, Helsby

THE END OF THE WORLD (PLANET POPSTAR)

It was a normal day until a black hole was in the sky. It swallowed me whole, I felt like I was in oblivion. Ten minutes later, the Waddle Dees went past me, then I ate a whole car. I was going 200 miles an hour! I landed in the Forgotten Land, well not forgotten now, found it! Lava, ice, grassland and even a funfair. But in the distance, I saw a Wild Edge with a ten-foot sword. I was terrified. Then it went dark, I felt weird... A bright light I had lost... I was defeated.

Rylee Thompson-Price (12)
Helsby High School, Helsby

THE KIND COMPANION

It was a normal day in the 1900s, until I saw a creepy house on a hill. I was interested in the house, so I went to go and explore it. When I got to the house it looked like it was abandoned. I crept into the house, there were cobwebs everywhere and one of them got in my mouth! I looked up the creaky staircase and saw a figure staring at me. I felt frozen. The shadow asked what my name was and was talking to me about what had happened to him. He was kind, and a ghost!

Scott Antrobus (12)
Helsby High School, Helsby

THE LION KING RETOLD

Pumbaa is travelling through the desert for his kind are in a war with the meerkats. Suddenly, Pumbaa sees a meerkat. They battle and they realise they do similar in battle so they stop and talk. Pumbaa learns the meerkat's name is Timon and he knows a way to an old war base where there is food. On their way they see trees and realise it is a jungle. They see a gigantic waterfall and they sprint to it, but before they get there they see a lion cub...

Cole Matthews (12)

Helsby High School, Helsby

MEDUSA

After I was framed for having an affair with Poseidon, Athena punished me with withering, slimy snakes as hair and anyone that looked at me would be frozen to stone. One day, this stupid boy came to my lair, saying he was going to kill me. I was just trying to be alone so I would not hurt anyone, but people wanted me dead because they accused me of witchcraft. I tried to explain what really happened but they just wanted to hunt me down and kill me.

Oliver Cavanagh (12)
Helsby High School, Helsby

I AM A TABLE

I have to tell you, I also get sad. They lean on me to eat, read and write. Sometimes they even draw on me. I am there for all their needs, but they just disrespect me. It is not like I can tell them or anyone. I just stand here in silence. Nobody knows I have feelings or even any thoughts. But I do and I hope this will stop people from disrespecting me. If you're reading this then please don't draw or write on me, only on paper. I am a table.

Grace Lynch (12)
Helsby High School, Helsby

PART OF THE CRUEL WORLD

Sheepishly, I crept behind her, her bursting red hair flowing in the wind. Her eyes widened and then melted when they met mine. What was she? Human or...? No, she looked half like a young woman but with a tail and fins! My mind blinked with visions of what I could do - the man who discovered a mermaid. I would grow to be rich, abundantly so, dictatorial.

"Let me help you," I offered.

Wait until people got a load of her...

Sophie Halsall-Cleworth (13)

Helsby High School, Helsby

WHAT DID I DO?

Nobody knew the truth about me. Nobody wanted to. Did anyone even care? All I wanted was to be happy, I didn't mean to cause chaos. I once had a love, someone to live and die for, but that all slipped away from me. I want to be free from this curse, but all that can save me is a ruby-red rose. So I locked myself away in my castle. See, I didn't mean to hurt anyone.

Isla Seymour (12)
Helsby High School, Helsby

ZERO TO HERO

Sweat seeped from every pore in his body. Heart pounding, his grasp around the vial tightened with his body trembling and mind racing. Flowing like a river throughout his mind one thought, *escape*. For his and humanity's only hope lay contained within thin glass in his sweaty palms. His heart heavy knowing after his brother they would stop at nothing to retrieve the cure. Voices grew louder, alarms shrieked as lights grew brighter; left with a choice at the edge. No family left, no hope, but one choice. The voices rushed up. He shut his eyes. And jumped...

James Bishop (14)
Penrice Academy, St Austell

MIRARI

For years, I've searched the Faust Mountains for a magic door. Before I embarked on my search, I was a blacksmith with a wife and three children. I had become a respected member of my community, but I threw my stable life away, for destiny, for adventure. When supplies were short, I returned to town, stealing what I got my hands on. The corpse in my former neighbour's house... All was worth it. According to legend, you open the door and will be granted what you deserve. Anything was better than languor. Knowing I deserve it, I open the door...

Adriana Curtis (13)
Penrice Academy, St Austell

MADE TO BE BAD

As a child, he was brought up with humiliation and intimidation. He thought it was right, and when people didn't want to be friends with him in elementary school, he acted like his parents. By high school he had big problems with aggression and if something went wrong, he would transfer his anger to people. During graduation, one of his 'friends' said what a terrible person he was. He got angry and beat him to death. Then he started attacking other people. Someone called the police. He was imprisoned for several years.

Zlata Skokova (14)
Penrice Academy, St Austell

ONE, TWO, THREE, I AM FREE...

As I roam the empty halls of the hospital, I hear on the speakers for patients to stay in their rooms.

I'm seen as a psycho maniac that needs locking up at the first chance, but my parents managed to get me into a mental institution to try and 'unlock the goodness within'. I try to tell people how it is not my fault that she fell off the bridge that night, but they just don't believe me.

Now I am out and can finally fulfil the destiny that people have written for me. Finally, I can get my revenge.

Tabitha Pinch (13)
Penrice Academy, St Austell

THE DEAR LIFE OF NYX JONES

Yes I am a villain and yes you might hate me, but let me share my story.

In my past, I had developed an urge to destroy. I wanted everyone to feel how I had felt when I saw my family killed right in front of my eyes. It was devastating and nobody had come to my rescue. Not even the so-called heroes of our world.

They were supposed to protect us and our powers from the world. People who used it for bad.

And now I use that power to make people feel what I felt...

Megan Jeffreys (12)
Penrice Academy, St Austell

WENDY AND THE TAKER

Where was the shadow taking me? "Peter, I can't leave my brothers," I tried to explain, with all my strength and power.
"It will be fine, Wendy, you'll be back for the morning."
I sighed, I stopped trying and let him take me. "Where are you taking me?"
"Neverland. Neverland, the land where you don't grow up, you stay young forever."
"Forever?"
"Well, as long as you stay there."
I gulped.
"Here we are!"
My eyes were filled with delight.
Bang!
"I... what's happening?"
"You're going nowhere ever again, you will never go back to your brothers..."

Katie Harvey (13)
Plympton Academy, Plympton

THE GRUFFALO - RETOLD

The mouse woke up one day at sunrise. He was feeling very tired and hungry so he wanted breakfast. The little mouse went for an early morning stroll in the deep dark woods where he'd heard the Gruffalo lived. Mouse walked deeper and deeper into the forest until he found a snake. "Snake," said Mouse, "have you seen the Gruffalo?"

Snake replied, "No I have not, but I've heard Fox knows."

"Fox," said the mouse, "do you know where the Gruffalo is?"

"Over there," said Fox.

Mouse eventually found the Gruffalo. "Hello Gruffalo, you're what I want for breakfast!"

Josh Buckley (12)

Plympton Academy, Plympton

REBIRTH OF THE DEVIL

They're gone now, he thought to himself. *They're gone.* Blood cloaked the grassy land and hills, with bodies mangled in broken poses, and shattered expressions to match. It's been hours, *they're gone now*, he thought once more. Arrows protruded from the ground around him and pierced the bodies of the dead. The once vast army was now a skeletal frame. Morgarath, Lord of the Mountains of Rain and Night, sat himself up and looked about the solemn massacre. Both armies were shattered, but Morgarath was still alive. However, Duncan remained. And the boy. "Not for much longer," he cackled maniacally.

Logan Conlon (12)
Plympton Academy, Plympton

CRETACEOUS PARK

It will be three years in two days from when my wife left me. Money has been tight since that dreadful night. I didn't understand why I could hear a siren. Suddenly, a man burst into the room and shouted, "We're evacuating the island!" The next second, he was gone.

Stumbling, I followed him outside. However, by the time I ventured out, he was being swallowed whole by a large carnivorous dinosaur. Shocked, terrified, frozen. I stood in place, hoping it wouldn't see me. "Metriacanthosaurus," I whispered. Instantly, the creature charged over and tossed me in the air...

Nathanael Wildgoose (12)
Plympton Academy, Plympton

THE TRUTH

It was one early morning and completely normal until a random figure appeared. The children were puzzled at who it was when a human wearing bright green appeared out of nowhere. He said, "You need to come with me now." He needed help so the children went with him. One of the children was afraid. "Where are we going?"
The human (Peter Pan) said, "A magical place." The children were over the moon. But little did they know, something was going to happen.
Peter said, "We need to stop Hook."
But when they arrived Peter did something shocking...

Jack Jones (13)
Plympton Academy, Plympton

BEAUTY LIES WITHIN

Appearances can be deceiving.

Belle's hair was long and she had eyes of sapphires. A smirk formed on her perfect lips as she banged on the oak door. The door slid open and she briskly edged inside, slipped her snow boots off and pounded up the first few steps before regaining herself and gliding softly. "Beast?" she called.

The Beast breathed heavily in the shadows. His face would be red if it weren't for the fur. He stepped out and Belle hugged him. Prince Adam within screamed in agony, blood gushing.

Gaston laughed. Belle laughed. They kissed passionately.

Megan Myles (13)

Plympton Academy, Plympton

THE TWISTED TALES OF CINDERELLA

My dreams had come true... Everything was going so well until Cinderella took my one opportunity for my evil mother to leave. She whispered into my ear with a hiss, "Kill him." She giggled loudly as she grabbed a knife and threatened me with only her eyes.

Slowly walking down the stairs to the happy couple, I started to grin. I shouldn't be like this, yet it excited me to kill.

I ran at him and sliced into his throat. Cinderella's heart-wrenching screams filled my ears with pleasure. What had I become? My mother's wishes murdered yet another innocent human.

Lyra Docton (13)
Plympton Academy, Plympton

ALADDIN AND THE EVIL WIZARD

Aladdin and the princess wandered through the endless desert, where they found a tiger mouth made out of rock-hard sand. As they looked in, they fell in the mouth and they found gold, diamonds, etc., but from the treasure came an evil laugh. A short evil wizard appeared and knocked them out.

Later, they woke up in cages and they saw blood all over the walls and Abu's dead body. Aladdin, in fear, shouted, "Why did you do this?"

"I've finally got you, Aladdin," said the wizard hysterically. The wizard leaned in with a knife. "Goodbye..."

Logan Findlay (12)

Plympton Academy, Plympton

SUPERMAN THE RAMPAGE

Zooming forward at the Earth in a huge meteor at the speed of sound, with only one objective, I smashed downwards, collapsing a skyscraper. Flying debris flew in all directions, hitting people on the street. I broke out and launched myself at the buildings and pulled them down, squashing all the survivors of the meteor collision. Laser beams and giant ice blocks were flying everywhere. Blood oozed down the streets and splattered up the walls. Thundering from city to city at the speed of light, I was unstoppable. Carnage and panic flew through the country and then the whole world.

Zac Stanton (11)
Plympton Academy, Plympton

LITTLE RED'S SECRET FRIEND

"Grandma, I have to tell you something. I'm sorry but I cannot hide it anymore. I have been hiding my best friend. His name is Charkey. Please don't freak out, he is a wolf. I know you are terrified of them but just meet him."
"Okay, I'll try my best."
"Here comes Charkey."
Charkey comes in and Grandma is a bit worried but so is Charkey. Grandma says, "Come in, let's have some tea." So he does and they are getting along. I am so happy, Grandma is getting over her fears and we all live happily ever after.

Riley Milton (13)
Plympton Academy, Plympton

MATILDA

Once upon a time, there was a little girl who had terrible parents. She once reached her dream of going to school. She had a very nice teacher but an unexpectedly rude head. Matilda found Miss Trunchbull's (the head) house and had to have a look. As soon as she entered she saw her and screamed like she never had before. Although, when she stopped, Miss Trunchbull smiled. She only wanted to talk to Matilda - she said the most shocking thing. The most unexpected words slipped out of her mouth, "I want to adopt you."
Matilda was confused, shocked, puzzled...

Eva-Lilie Smith (12)
Plympton Academy, Plympton

CHILD MUNCHER (HANSEL AND GRETEL)

Dreams had come true when two children, Hansel and Gretel, arrived at the magnificent house. Sweets, chocolate and candy filled the walls and rooms of the home, luring the children towards her. Unfortunately, this was a bad case for them. Being misled from their tracks, they arrived. Hansel and Gretel ran towards the house, eating the food, when she came crawling out. Her grotty hands grabbed them both and dragged them inside. When they awoke, they were being buried in a furnace. Passing out again, they never woke up. All of the witch's treats then were made of their flesh.

Willow Stephenson (13)
Plympton Academy, Plympton

THE CROWN HAS FALLEN

"Rapunzel, Rapunzel, let down your hair!" Flynn yelled. Rapunzel was too busy reading to let her hair flow to the ground. As Flynn climbed, he thought about the crown and how rich he would be after he sold it.

When he reached the top, Rapunzel yelped and jumped away from the ledge. Grabbing a frying pan, she shouted, "Stay back!" As he tried to speak, she hit the pan across his face, causing blood to slip down his cheek. He collapsed and she brought it down on him again, smashing his skull. The last thing he heard was, "Leave now!"

Niamh Roberts (13)
Plympton Academy, Plympton

RAPUNZEL'S MADNESS

Rapunzel stood over her mother's corpse, blood still dripping from the sword of glass, laughing, uncontrollably happy with the fact that the witch was dead. Dread slowly crept in now, realising she had nobody to talk to and no food. Over the next few days, she resorted to eating rats and licking moisture off the tower walls. The colour of her face had vanished. She had killed the prince, believing him to be a hallucination sent to torment her. Eventually, the rats ran out with only her mother's rotting corpse left. Slowly, Rapunzel walked over and began to feast.

Miles Bradbury-Webb (13)
Plympton Academy, Plympton

DR FACILIER AND THE SHADOWS

"I have some friends on the other side."
Hello, welcome to my voodoo palace. Before we start, I have to tell you about me. One night, I'd just left my house when everything went dark. Voices spoke, but the only thing there were shadows. They were independent from bodies. They said, "You are our prisoner." A giant skull opened. I felt I was to become the most powerful being in the world. First thing, take as many souls as possible before my friends take me. So how would you like to meet them?
"I have friends on the other side."

Mollie Lavers (12)
Plympton Academy, Plympton

MATILDA TORTURE

Once, there was a girl called Matilda. Matilda was a lovely girl and was extremely smart. Matilda had an amazing family and amazing friends and overall, an amazing life. Except for school. In school she had a teacher called Miss Honey. Miss Honey hated children, she practically tortured the children.

One day, when Matilda got to school, the most tragic thing happened. One student wore a hairstyle that wasn't allowed in school, so Miss Honey picked her up and threw her across the road! This caused the girl's parents to sue the school. It never reopened.

Mason Vosper (12)

Plympton Academy, Plympton

JULIET AND JULIET

Once, there was a very happy couple, Romeo and Juliet.
"Oh, I am so happy being with thou," Juliet said.
"I feel the same," Romeo replied.
After a few winters, Juliet met up with Romeo's sister. Juliet was so taken by her, and so was she. This was the beginning of a perfect relationship. Juliet tried to find a way to ditch Romeo. She went to him and said, "I'm sorry, but I found out I'm going to pass away." Then she lay on the floor till he left. Then Juliet got up and ran away with his sister, Juliet.

Pixie Elliott (12)
Plympton Academy, Plympton

LITTLE RED RIDING HOOD GONE WRONG

"Give this to your nan," she said to the girl.

So she walked through the forest to her nan's house. When she reached her house she knocked on the door. "Come in," a deep voice growled. The girl's nan looked very hairy with sharp teeth and nails. "Come closer," her nan said. So she did.

Without warning, her nan sprang out of bed... but she was a wolf! The girl screeched loudly. The wolf was viciously swiping at her. A lumberjack barged in the door and started swinging his axe at the wolf... but it devoured them both.

Heidi Mudge (12)
Plympton Academy, Plympton

JACKIE AND JILL: A TWISTED TALE

Jill, the CEO of Aquaplant, a water filtration business, with her wife Jackie, awoke to the worst day of her life. She uncovered a box of items belonging to dead people - Jackie was a serial killer! Jill decided to confront her wife at the peak of the tallest hill in the city.

Trembling at the revelations, Jackie denied all accusations. Both furious, they fought. Jackie plummeted off the hill and Jill went tumbling after. Blood smeared on the rocks as Jackie split the crown of her skull. Horrified at the sight of the love of her life, dead, Jill turned pale.

Heidi Bassett (14)
Plympton Academy, Plympton

BIRD'S EYE PERSPECTIVE ON PADDINGTON

When my husband passed away in the navy twenty years ago, I had been trying to keep everything in ship-shape condition. I was for a long time successful, but that became harder when a fuzzy bear came into my life. I had been working for the Brown family for fifteen years at this point, and one day everything changed. I distracted that silly policeman with a drinking competition and launched that stupid, evil Montgomery woman off the top of the National Museum, with a trapdoor. The whole family loves Paddington Bear, Mrs and Mr Brown, Judy and dear old Johnathan.

Jack Welsman (12)
Plympton Academy, Plympton

THE WOLF FUR JACKET

Once upon a time, Little Red Riding Hood was walking to her grandma's house with lots of tasty snacks. What she didn't know was that a wolf had entered the house and pretended to be Grandma. When she got there she noticed that something was off. "What big teeth you have!"
"All the better to eat you with!" shouted the wolf.
However, Little Red Riding Hood didn't look scared. She had an ominous smile on her face. Suddenly, she pulled out a gun from her hood and killed the wolf. "You will make a nice fur jacket!"

Tommy Lane (13)
Plympton Academy, Plympton

WAR OF THE WORLDS 1938

Boots smash across the floor, orders are shouted across the square. The mechanic hum of vehicles as they come to life fills the air with the smell of petrol. Hanz clambers into the back of the truck, next to him are his fellow soldiers there is little talk. This is the first time they've entered combat. They are being scrambled to bolster the defence of Munich from the mountains.

As they enter the city a deafening roar is heard. On the horizon a massive metal warlord is carved into the crimson silhouette. The smash of artillery drowns out all thinking.

Eddie Keaney (12)
Plympton Academy, Plympton

RAPUNZEL, RAPUNZEL, LET GO OF YOUR HAIR

It was the big day! Rapunzel rushed to get ready. She yanked her dress out of her dresser and put it on. It was her stylish show today. She was worried about it but she had it. She needed someone to judge her outfit so she called Flynn. "Come 'ere now!"

"Okay," said Flynn, and he hopped into his Ferrari and drove to her tower. He crashed into the trees until he got there and Rapunzel shouted, "Gerup." So he did. He climbed up, then something terrible happened to her hair... It ripped off! They both fell from the tower...

Toby Kent (11)
Plympton Academy, Plympton

THE PALACE IS ON FIRE

The sun was setting when disaster struck. Belle and the Beast were dancing the night away with Mrs Potts and Lumiere, having the time of their lives. The graceful couple danced on top of a small table in the middle of the ballroom when Belle tripped over and landed on top of the round table, sending Mrs Potts and Lumiere high up into the air. Lumiere managed to grab onto the gold chandelier above, however, Mrs Potts was smashed. Lumiere was devasted and fuming, which led him to setting the drapes alight, setting the palace and everything inside on fire...

Lewis Talmage (13)
Plympton Academy, Plympton

THE GRUFFALO'S DEMISE

The relief you felt when the mouse revealed how scary he was almost made you faint. Who knew the Gruffalo could be so overruled by a small mouse?

"I know the shock you must feel."

What was the mouse on about? Surely the smile on your face proved otherwise?

"Why don't you come to my home for some tea? We could talk over our feelings?"

What harm could it do? Besides, it would be nice to have a friend to relate to, right? So off you went.

As Snake peered in, he saw Mouse eating lumpy stew alone. Wait, alone?

Sienna Bell (12)

Plympton Academy, Plympton

THE THREE BIG WOLVES

I couldn't believe my eyes. A pig chasing three wolves! The first wolf ran into his straw house. The pig said, "Don't make me come in there! 3, 2, 1..." The pig charged into the house and ate the first wolf.

The second wolf ran into his wood house. The pig said, "Don't make me come in there! 3, 2, 1..." He charged into the second pig's house and ate him.

The third wolf ran into his brick house, The pig said, "Don't make me come in there! 3, 2, 1..." He charged at it and failed, and fell, dying.

Tyler King (13)
Plympton Academy, Plympton

RAPUNZEL DIES, A TWISTED TALE

Nobody knew the truth about me. Rapunzel wasn't keeping me young, the child in my basement was. As soon as I realised this, Rapunzel was no longer needed. I concocted a plan, an evil plan nonetheless. Rapunzel would be dead by tomorrow.

I had collected the poison berries on my travels yesterday and I mixed them in with her food. As Rapunzel casually ate her meal, I watched, waiting for her to drop dead. Sure enough, with two bites left, Rapunzel dropped off her chair onto the floor. Feeling victorious, I triumphed as she took her last breath.

Isla Ashford (13)
Plympton Academy, Plympton

URSULA

Nobody knows the truth about me. Everyone assumes I've always been evil, but they're wrong. It wasn't until the age of 16, after I had my first heartbreak. I always dreamt of my happily ever after, but after my heartbreak I never found anyone special. I thought if I had a better voice someone would fall in love with me again. So I stole Ariel's voice and her fiancé Eric. I was finally going to get my happily ever after.

When Poseidon came to kill me I tried to explain I just wanted to be loved. Then everything went black...

Olivia Smith (13)
Plympton Academy, Plympton

A NEW HAIRCUT

At first, it just seemed like another typical day in the village. Work was normal, my servants still listened to my every command. Yet, it quickly changed. A peasant had come knocking, questioning me about a voice from a tower. It was home to the village's slimiest thief. I explained her actions and why she was locked up, yet he still tried to persist then stormed out. I went to the tower, awaiting the peasant's inevitable appearance. Sure enough, he tried to climb her hair, but a snip and a cackle later, he was sprawled across the wet grass!

Jake Cox (13)
Plympton Academy, Plympton

GOLDILOCKS AND THE THREE WOLVES

I lifted my head up and opened my eyes to an unknown place. The door opened and three wolves appeared. My jaw dropped and I wondered why they were here.

"You're awake," said one of them.

I tried to remember how I got here, but all I could remember was everything turning black. Where was I? Was I getting out alive? I tried getting out but my hands and feet were stuck. I started to scream.

"Are you ready to die, Goldi?" one of them said.

I rustled around again for any luck escaping but then all went black...

Isla Young (13)

Plympton Academy, Plympton

MR SMILE

Detective log #47. It's been a week since they found the body under the bridge. So far we've identified the victim as Corius Herrordes. We visited the victim's brother, Jones. When we got there he was acting nervous as if he was hiding something. We asked him if he knew anything and he said he saw a person with his brother when he left, but he couldn't remember who. We asked about a smile marking carved into the victim's mouth.
We found a location. I went there. I was knocked out. When I woke, I was wearing a smiley mask...

Maddox Healy (12)
Plympton Academy, Plympton

THE THREE LITTLE KIDS

"Bye Mum," the kids said, going to build homes. The first kid built one out of chocolate, so he could have a snack anytime. The second found a hay bail, it was as strong as can be. The third used steel so it could survive storms and bad weather.

A wolf came along, very hungry, and saw the chocolate house, so he gobbled it up. The kid screamed, "Argh!" and ran to the hay house. He went in just as it was blown away. "Argh!"

They ran to their brother's, but the wolf couldn't blow it down or eat it!

Charlie Gibson (12)

Plympton Academy, Plympton

JURASSIC PARK: EMBRYOS GONE MISSING

Red, blue and white, the gaudy colours on the aerosol can reminded Denis of the American flag. Denis Nedry was admiring the can when he was told to work at Jurassic Park for two weeks.

When he was working he noticed the guests by the tyrannosaurus paddock. He turned off the power and went to get something - embryos. He got them and got to a jeep and sped off. John Hammond regretted hiring Denis.

Denis soon crashed into a waterfall. He tried getting out and succeeded. Soon a dilophosaur came but Denis sped off. Biosyn now had dinosaurs...

George Hillyer (13)
Plympton Academy, Plympton

BEAUTY AND THE BEAST

Far, far away, over the rooftops and hills, there was a small village where not many people lived. In the smallest house of all in the village, lived a troublesome beast who was always getting into trouble. The mighty beast was isolated in his home because everyone hated him. He was the most vicious animal of all time. The murderous beast had killed hundreds, so the troublesome beast was locked away and no one ever saw him. Till this day...

He came out of his house and made new friends. The beast turned into a nice person who everyone liked.

Maya Chapple (12)
Plympton Academy, Plympton

THE HUNTING

Late at night, little Sophie, with her teddy in her basket, kept walking to her grandma's little hut. She kept hearing howling all around her, she was scared. She kept walking faster and faster until she was bolting across the woodland. In a few minutes, she arrived at her grandmother's, but she could see fur all over her. Sophie walked closer to her unsuspecting murderer. As the furry creature tried to grab Sophie, its nightgown fell off and it showed a wolf with bloody teeth!

Just as Sophie was about to be eaten... *bang!*

Lucas Mackney (12)
Plympton Academy, Plympton

CINDERELLA - DRIVEN TO MURDER

Cinderella was but a girl, tormented for her looks and forced to clean for them. Tears trickled down her cheeks as she spoke, "Please stop this."
Her comment was ignored and they spat out, "No! You work under us, at least we took you in! Now prepare our dresses." They left and Cinderella had a thought. What if she stole one of the dresses? So she did that exactly and thought it would be better to get rid of any suspicion, so she murdered her stepsisters with a mop. She was sick of her life, then went on her way.

Sam Dado (12)
Plympton Academy, Plympton

CAPTAIN HOOK

Peter Pan walked up to the tree. He grabbed five fairies and put them on the floor. He stomped on them, making them turn into glitter. Captain Hook watched it. He ran up to Peter and shouted, "You killed the fairies!"
Peter Pan ran and found a sharp stick. Captain Hook got his hook ready. They fought. Captain Hook slashed Peter with his hook. Peter Pan fell down. Captain Hook kicked Peter and spat on him. "How dare you kill the fairies!" He grabbed Peter Pan at the neck and threw him against a tree, then tied him up.

James Burdon (13)
Plympton Academy, Plympton

THE GIRL WITH THE BLOOD-RED HOOD

Once upon a time, Jenny was walking to her grandma's house. The wolf tried to help her, knowing her grandma had been replaced by an evil twin. However, the girl didn't believe him.

As the girl ran to her grandma's house, she was immediately offered food, but it was filled with poison. When she turned the food down, her grandma threw a knife at her. She ducked and the knife hit the wolf. The girl happily took the knife out of the wolf and threw it at her 'grandma', killing her. She then walked away calmly and happily.

Molly Howe (12)

Plympton Academy, Plympton

TRYING TO HELP

I was just walking through a forest when I spotted a small girl. She seemed lost. I carefully approached. "Are you lost, dear?"
She screamed in terror and ran, dropping some medicine. It had an address to return it. The address was a small cottage. Little did I know the girl in red was in the bushes. I saw her running to a lumberjack's house. How strange.
I knocked on the cottage door and an old lady opened it. As I handed the medicine to her I felt a sharp pain in my back. "I was just trying to help!"

Liam Talmage (13)
Plympton Academy, Plympton

THE WOLF WINS

Lost in the moment, her body was shocked. As she lay there still, a wisp of wind blew her hair and she flicked it back. There was the sound of branches breaking, the wolf appeared. Looking at him she was thinking to herself how scared she was.

"Hi, I'm going to eat you!" cried the wolf.

"No you're not!" yelled the girl in horror (in her head she was scared, she didn't show it though).

The wolf's mouth was dripping with his spit as she thought to herself, *golly, this is the end...*

April Howitt (13)

Plympton Academy, Plympton

MY REAL STORY

Nobody knew the truth about me. I had a daughter before Rapunzel. She's all I think about.

I got home from picking berries and Rapunzel was gone. I couldn't believe her! After all these years of being looked after she just left! I started looking for her around the village and found out she and a man were walking towards the town. If she uncovered who I really was I was screwed. There were loads of massive crowds in the kingdom. I put my disguise on and started looking for her. I found her! I finally had a daughter again...

Freya Edwards-Ede (12)
Plympton Academy, Plympton

THE THREE LITTLE PIGS

It was the big day, the three little pigs were going to leave, until their clingy mother decided to keep them home. The three pigs argued with the mum but she insisted they stay. Then eventually, they heard a big puff and *boom!* The house was in ruins. The pigs trembled in fear and tried to run. Their efforts were ruined because their mother dragged them towards the wolf. The pigs squealed with fear as they were gobbled down one by one. The wolf gave a big belch and he thanked the mother for her services which were magnificent!

Oliver Eastman (12)
Plympton Academy, Plympton

THE END OF CINDERELLA

As he put the shoe onto her foot, he let out a gasp; to his disappointment, it didn't fit.

A few years later and they were both happily married, or so we thought. Prince Charming never wanted to marry Cinderella, yet he had no choice. Because of this, he abused her daily, physically and verbally. Cinderella had had enough and jumped from the top floor of the palace, which killed her. The prince couldn't bear the guilt and the blame, so he had to give up his crown and he ran away. Who knows if he is alive or dead.

Tayla Madavan (13)
Plympton Academy, Plympton

THE SNAKE'S STORY

I awoke to a rustling outside my lair. I slithered over and saw a mouse walk past. Feeling hungry, I followed him, getting closer. As I was about to lunge, I heard a thud and shot back into a bush. A creature had emerged from the trees. It and the mouse spoke then off the mouse walked. The creature followed it and I followed them. Twice they stopped to terrify an owl then a fox. Eventually, they stopped again and I slunk closer. Then the creature left. This was my chance. I lunged forwards, killing the mouse. Then I feasted.

Reuben Lamude (12)
Plympton Academy, Plympton

THE LITTLE SIREN

Ariel let her tears fall from her eyes. She couldn't believe that the prince had chosen Ursula over her. To add to her misery, her time with legs had ended.

She swam out from the beach, the place of her rejection, to her stack, not far from the cliffs. It was night now and she began to sing a mournful tune. She opened her eyes in a panic. She realised her song had lured the sailors to crash their ship against the rocks. She grinned. If she couldn't be happy then she would make sure nobody else could ever be.

Isabel Allen (13)

Plympton Academy, Plympton

THE THREE PIGS CONQUER THE WORLD

Nobody knew the truth about us. We were known as the golden pigs growing up. It needed to change. 19 villages and the loss of our mother and father, we needed revenge on the wolves. One village remained, 25 wolves and 3 pigs, we would take them down.

Wolf Woods is where we arrived. We made our way from left to right, killing all the wolves that were around. We came to the last house. Our bodies fell through the chimney, covering all areas of the house. We cornered the wolf in a room. It was us three against him...

Ruby Friend (13)

Plympton Academy, Plympton

INCY'S FINAL SPLASH-ABOUT

Us raindrops knew many land people. We usually drenched them all with our naughty schemes. However, one escaped us every time. His name was Incy Wincy. He was a pesky spider. For years we raced down to him, hoping to soak him. We never did. He was also too fast and nifty and evaded us. One day, though, the tables turned.

It was a dark sky and the clouds dispatched us. We saw Incy sleeping atop his drain, an easy target. So we surrounded his web. I hit him first. He shuddered awake, not realising the end loomed...

Ethan Sterland (12)

Plympton Academy, Plympton

CINDERELLA

It was the big day. Everyone was filled with joy and happiness as the prince finally wanted to find his love from the ball that night. Cinderella felt relieved she was going to find her way out of her miserable life as a slave for her stepmum.

Suddenly, a knock on the door was heard. She was so excited she couldn't help but smile as the sound of horses travelled through her ears.

First was Cinderella to try it, but something was wrong, it didn't fit. But it did the ugly sisters. This was impossible!

Lilia Abbott (13)
Plympton Academy, Plympton

THE TALE OF THE WOLF AND THE CEREMONY

The wolf's tribe was located in the woods. There was a member turning into an adult and in this tribe there was a ceremony where a new adult had to capture and eat three pigs.

"I must find three pigs," he muttered.

He went on a hunt to find the porksters. They had all built houses from different materials. He needed the pigs so he blew two down until they all went to the brick house, which he smashed down with a hammer. He grabbed them and roasted them over a fire. He was accepted as an adult.

Mason Ebanks (12)

Plympton Academy, Plympton

LITTLE RED RIDING HOOD AND THE WEREWOLF

The bloodthirsty werewolf was rampaging throughout the city, destroying everything in its path. It was fierce and worst of all it was hungry.

A girl wearing a beautiful, silky, smooth cloak ran through roads and jumped across cars. As the wolf pursued her, it threw the vehicles in its path out of the way. It was slowly edging closer to the girl when she headed into a deep, dark forest. She didn't even dare to look back, and then it lost her, so she sat behind a tree relieved. But she was then discovered...

Dylan Fuller (12)

Plympton Academy, Plympton

THE BLOODY TOWER

She lay there. Strong contact with the stone floor. A series of creaks flooded her ears as a rectangular-shaped head popped up at her window. Hair spread across the floor, she sat up. Thuds louder than thunder as the prince ran across and removed it, laughing as he jumped out of the window in a hurry, the hair swept over his arm. A hand came up to cover her face at the same minute as the vines from the tower walls started to crawl onto the floor of the tower and wrap quickly around her neck, tighter and tighter...

Erin Shepherd (13)
Plympton Academy, Plympton

SOGGY GINGERBREAD MAN

Once upon a time, the gingerbread man was running through Drury Lane after visiting the good old Muffin Man. As the gingerbread man was running out of Drury Lane, he emerged into a large field with a small river running through it. The gingerbread man was racing along the stones beside the river until one of the stones slipped from under him and he fell straight into the river. The gingerbread man splashed about, screaming for help until he was all soggy and falling apart. The gingerbread man was never seen again.

Emily Scott-Davies (13)
Plympton Academy, Plympton

THE WOLF FROM THE THREE LITTLE PIGS

Nobody knew the truth about the wolf. He lost his dad when he was three. When he went to school, the three little pigs bullied him and now he wanted to get revenge.

The three little pigs set off to build houses and the wolf followed the first. Once his house was built he blew it down and ate him. He then blew down the second pig's house and chased him to the third pig's house. The second pig still got eaten. The wolf tried to blow the brick house down but he climbed down the chimney and got stuck...

Zachary Bamford (13)
Plympton Academy, Plympton

RAPUNZEL'S TWISTED LIFE!

Rapunzel was on her way to school on the bus. She sat with her friends Max and Luke. They arrived at school and raced each other to get chocolate.

Once they had made their way to MU1 they got working on their concert. This is the life Rapunzel lived.

As the big concert came around, she was about to go on but then the power went out. The power came back and she was on stage. Rapunzel was shocked by a standing ovation after she played. She walked off stage to cool down and watched the Year 11s going on.

Ellie Pritchard (12)

Plympton Academy, Plympton

QUEEN'S DEATH SENTENCE

The plan was in motion. After the dwarves left Snow White so they could work, the evil queen came to see the girl. But there was a problem in the horrid plan; when Snow was living with her the queen had sleeptalked and the plan flowed out of her mouth to Snow's ears. So when the queen dropped by, Snow knew it was a murder plot! Snow pretended to feel faint and asked the hag to get her some water. When the villain's back was turned, Snow switched the apples in the basket. The queen bit in, then died.

Sophia Thrift (12)
Plympton Academy, Plympton

THE CRAZY WOLF ABOMINATION

The third little piggy made his house out of bricks. The wolf said he would blow the house down, so he huffed and puffed and blew, but nothing happened. So he went down the chimney and landed in a scalding hot cauldron. As he boiled, he became a fleshy abomination of what used to be a wolf. Blood filled the cauldron, but he didn't die. The third piggy screamed in terror as the abomination moaned a deep tune, "The world is much better here, you will never be lonely."
Then the world faded.

Logan Kirk (12)
Plympton Academy, Plympton

HOOK

Nobody knew the truth about me. Peter Pan is the true villain. Everyone would hate him if they knew what he did to me and my crew.

One day aboard my ship, a storm was closing in. I knew we must take shelter in headquarters, but I made a grave mistake and thought we could withstand it. We stayed on deck and sailed further into the eye of the storm. Suddenly, screams were heard. I turned around and a boy dressed in green stood there covered in blood, surrounded by my dead crew. His name was Peter Pan.

Willow Aitchison (13)
Plympton Academy, Plympton

GOLDILOCKS AND THE THREE BEARS

It was a normal day until the three bears had had enough of the horrid girl. The three bears came up with a deadly plan. After walking miles, they found the girl's house which had been left to rot in the middle of the dark forest. The three bears tumbled in the house and were greeted with a feast of food. They stuffed their faces until there was none left. Then Daddy Bear put poison in some more food and waited until the girl woke up. She ate the food... "She's dead!" Then they ate her!

Will Ford (13)
Plympton Academy, Plympton

GOLDILOCKS AND THE THREE BEARS

It was a sunny day when a little girl was skipping in the forest. She skipped to the middle of the forest and came across a small cottage. She walked up to it and entered the house. She looked around the house to make sure it was empty. She came across the kitchen and stole food from the fridge and the cupboards. She entered a bedroom and got into the bed and went to sleep.

About one hour later, she woke and left the house and some bears walked up to her and kidnapped her! She was never seen again.

Faith Walsh (13)
Plympton Academy, Plympton

RAPUNZEL AND KING BOB

Once upon a time, there was a king called Bob. He lived in a kingdom called Bobland. He was a good king, everyone liked him.

One day, he was doing some yoga when his servant came in and told the king his daughter had been stolen. So off he went to find her. He was in the woods and he came across a stone tower. He tried to open the door but couldn't. Rapunzel said, "Help!" So he climbed up to get her, using her hair. He saved her and took her back to the kingdom. King Bob, the hero.

Jamie Boyes (12)
Plympton Academy, Plympton

THE END OF NEVERLAND

Once upon a time, in a land far from here called Neverland, Captain Hook, his teeth chattering with fear, was thinking about how he could save those helpless children from Peter Pan. Once they all turned 13, it was over, Peter would have killed them and used them for more pixie dust so he could rule the entire Neverland and then soon, London. But, Captain Hook had one last trick up his hook to save Neverland and destroy Peter Pan once and for all. That was to take away the source of his pixie dust...

Rhys Slade (13)
Plympton Academy, Plympton

I KILLED MY SHEEP

Dear Diary,

I made a mistake today. I stole my father's gun and all the sheep tried to run. Angry and mad, I ran to the barn, gun beneath my arm. Ringing pierced the air. I screamed and didn't care. Blood poured over the heaps of fur and weakly did they purr. Little Bo Peep has killed the sheep and I don't know where to hide them. My mind would scream at me, I dropped to my knees. My dress was in a mess, my sanity became less and less. Help me please, my head kept trying to tease.

Bethany Prowse (13)

Plympton Academy, Plympton

THE MOUSE'S END

When the mouse finds the Gruffalo he is hiding behind a tree. First, they go to the fox, who gets scared and runs off. Then they go to the snake, but the owl is watching. The owl swoops in and grabs the mouse. The Gruffalo, who is scared, ducks and runs for cover. The mouse is released from the owl's claws and the mouse falls right into the snake's mouth. The snake gulps once and then that is it for the mouse. The snake and the owl had planned this all out beforehand, in their secret base.

George Adkins (11)
Plympton Academy, Plympton

THE BEAST TURNS

Beauty and the Beast were having a beautiful relationship. But there was a knight that was jealous and would always send Beauty love gifts and the Beast did not like this and ended up hitting the knight. They fought and the Beast won, but Beauty was very angry and sad at the Beast. Beauty really liked how the knight showed her love; the Beast loved her very much but would not show the love. The knight snuck in and kissed Beauty. The Beast ended up killing Beauty as the knight tried to save her...

Charlie Matthews (13)

Plympton Academy, Plympton

BEAUTY AND THE BEAST

One day, the Beast was walking in the woods, when he heard crying. He found who was crying, it was a girl called Belle. The Beast fell in love. The Beast and Belle had a date and became a thing.

A few months passed and it was their anniversary. It got very late and Belle was drunk. She took some medicine which made her turn into a savage person. She flung her cup and glass went everywhere. She grabbed a knife and sliced the Beast's head off. There was blood everywhere. She just laughed.

Elana Taylor (12)
Plympton Academy, Plympton

HANSEL AND GRETEL ARE MY BREAKFAST

The plan was in motion, I'd set the trail of treats leading them right to their doom. I heard cracks of wood getting louder and louder. The oven was nice and hot ready for cooking my meal, it was perfect. Then a knock at the door, yes! It worked! I welcomed them in and gave them a cookie with a sleeping serum in, then got ready to put the children in the oven. Oh, wait! They'd woken up and they were attacking me! I only put a drop of sleeping serum in, I should have put two! Oh no, help!

Hayden Watters (13)
Plympton Academy, Plympton

THE THREE LITTLE WOLVES

Once upon a time, the three little wolves got too big for their mother's home, so they went off and got materials to build their own homes. They finished their houses. One was a stick house, but a pig came and set it on fire so the wolf ran to the second house, the brick house. The pig tried and tried to destroy it, then he had a plan. He got a bulldozer with a crane and took the whole house up! Then they ran to the last modern house and the pig said to the wolf, "This is nice!"

Harlee Mutch (12)
Plympton Academy, Plympton

BUZZ'S STORY

Buzz's dreams had come true until one day Buzz had a new neighbour called Sid. He was a cruel little boy who loved to destroy toys. Buzz had a plan to scare Sid so much he would run away. All he needed was his friends to help, they agreed. All the toys entered Sid's house and hid, but their plan backfired because one toy had been caught by the dog which alerted Sid. Sid managed to get all the toys. He took them to his dark room; as soon as they went in no one saw them again.

Oliver Ewing (13)
Plympton Academy, Plympton

THE THREE BUILDERS

It was a big day for the building community, to see who made the best material for a house. The first opponent was Jamie. He made his house out of straw so Bob, the head of building, brought a hammer to see if the house was stable. He got his hammer and swung it and Jamie's house was knocked down, so he was out. Next was Scott, he made his out of wood. Bob swung his hammer and he was out. Finally, it was Harry, he made it out of bricks. Bob swung... it didn't break so Harry won!

Harry Maloney (11)
Plympton Academy, Plympton

THE LONELY WOLF

Once upon a time, the lonely wolf was strolling around the silent wood when he saw a lonely girl. He couldn't believe his eyes. As he approached her she got scared and ran home. Nobody knew the truth about him.

All of a sudden, he spotted a quiet house. He approached and entered and saw an old woman needing help, she was scared of him. Then Red Riding Hood entered and the wolf ran away in embarrassment.

From that day on, the lonely wolf was still always lonely. Poor wolf!

Oliver Batten (12)
Plympton Academy, Plympton

THE TWISTED PUSS

One morning, I woke from my sleep to find I was a dog. A Shiba Inu to be exact. At least I was still ginger. But I was worried because I was meant to be doing a 'cat' walk on stage with my boots, and now I wasn't a cat. Oh well, I was no longer a participant. I had a massive urge to jump into the river, but I hate water! I couldn't stand on my two legs, I would have to wear dog shoes instead of my boots. *Oh well, I'm pretty sure it will wear off tomorrow...*

Joshua Pardoe (12)

Plympton Academy, Plympton

THE MAN FROM THE BEANSTALK

Nobody knows the truth about me, everyone thinks that I'm some evil, bloodthirsty giant, but that's not me at all! I've been trapped in the clouds for decades! The only wish I have is to see and explore the world below. I thought the wish had come true when a tall beanstalk emerged from the clouds and I saw a tiny man climb up and hop on my window. I thought he was there to take me to the world below. Oh, how wrong I was. I had never felt so betrayed up until that moment.

Alex Piora (13)
Plympton Academy, Plympton

WHAT HAPPENED IF MERIDA WAS FORCED TO MARRY

I took his hand and he took mine as we said our vows whilst the kingdoms were screaming with joy. I hated it.

Soon after, I ran to the witch and demanded a permanent spell be put on my mother. She grew taller and hairier and roared. My father heard and rushed to save me. He impaled her with a mighty sword. Blood went everywhere. She was gone.

I met my husband upstairs as he lazily sat in bed. I offered him a drink and he greedily gulped it down and slept... never to wake.

Ava Mason (13)
Plympton Academy, Plympton

ALICE IN WONDERLAND

It was a normal day, I was just walking and fell into a hole. I slid down it like a slide, although I got cut on the way down. It felt like claws were slicing into me. I reached the bottom to find a little white rabbit, it smiled at me then attacked me! I was able to escape it through a door and ran into a lady who called herself the Queen of Hearts. She looked at me like I had done it on purpose but of course I hadn't. She called for her guards. "Off with her head!"

Lizzy Griffiths (12)

Plympton Academy, Plympton

LITTLE RED RIDING HOOD, THE WOLF'S POV

It was a bright sunny day. I was out scavenging for food, but then I saw a small innocent girl wearing a chequered skirt. My mouth drooled, I was hungry. I followed her and realised she was going to her granny's house, so I ran ahead as I had an amazing plan. I kicked the door down and quickly ate Granny. I put her clothes on and sat in her bed waiting for the little girl to appear. Finally, she did and she came up to me with a smile on her face. I took my chance and ate her!

Isabela Kingdom (13)
Plympton Academy, Plympton

168

THE BFG'S DARK SIDE

Crash! I woke. I heard the BFG talking to himself. I rose up and hid behind a can. I saw a plan on the chalkboard. The title was 'Plan to Kill Sophie'. I was so confused. I kept having flashbacks of him saying to me that the other giants were bad. It was all a lie. He probably kept me here to study me.

Out of nowhere, a random giant stormed in and grabbed me. He tried to run out of the house, but the BFG knocked me onto the floor. All I saw was darkness...

Elika Gallais-Worth (13)

Plympton Academy, Plympton

THE THREE LITTLE PIGS

It was a normal day until the three little pigs were on a walk. Suddenly, they spotted a wolf by himself. The pigs chased the wolf over the mountains; they chased him to a straw house to trap him but he blew it down and ran off again. The pigs chased the wolf through the forest to a stick house and tried to trap him again but he blew it down and ran. Eventually, he ran into a brick house and tried to blow it down too but couldn't, so the pigs set it on fire. The wolf died.

Harvey Llewellyn (13)
Plympton Academy, Plympton

THE TRUTH OF MOANA

I have to tell you, my life isn't what you think. Every day, my dad makes me take weakening pills, but I don't care anymore, I'm going out there. I hop on my boat, weaker than ever and off I go. My boat crashes against the waves as I get deeper. I find this island and I see a man sitting. He asks for a ride so I let him. The waves get bigger. Suddenly a wave gobbles the boat. I see he is trying to find me, but it is too late. I feel my weak body sink underwater.

Millie Webb (12)
Plympton Academy, Plympton

MATILDA

A girl called Matilda had horrible parents called Bob and Jan. They put her in a school with only one mean teacher, her name was Miss Honey but then a nice teacher joined called Miss Trunchbull. Miss Trunchbull was so nice, she helped with anything. She told Matilda one day, "Matilda, come here, I have something to tell you... I am adopting you!"
"Yay!"
Miss Honey was shocked when she heard about this, but then she started to turn nice...

Lucas Canning (12)
Plympton Academy, Plympton

FARQUAAD'S VICTORY AND AN OGRE'S DEFEAT

The Lord told me he had a job I could do, it was hunting an ogre named Shrek. It seemed pointless and too much of a drag really, but the king paid well for the job.

I arrived at the location not far from town. It was a simple cabin with a mudbath around it. My prey walked out, he was quite slow. I aimed my bow at his eye, it hit him. He screamed in pain. I dashed towards him, sword in hand and a moment later I aimed my sword at his neck and cleaved his head off.

Owen Collings (13)
Plympton Academy, Plympton

THE WOLF'S MASSACRE

People thought I was a normal wolf until they saw me. They saw the evilness in my eyes.
I lived in the forest. Three pigs walked past, I licked my lips. Once I killed them they would be my breakfast, lunch and dinner. I jumped out and chased them. Two of them went into a hay house because they didn't want to be alone. I grabbed a torch and burnt the house down. The other went into a brick house. I broke the door down and ripped him apart, then walked home.

Kaleb Dolling (13)
Plympton Academy, Plympton

RAPUNZEL WITH A TWIST

Once upon a time, there was a girl with long, beautiful, golden hair. But this girl was trapped in a tall, eerie tower, with an evil mother.

One day, the mother went out to get a gun. When she was out, Rapunzel discovered the truth that she had been kidnapped at birth. So when her mother came back, Rapunzel put her plan into motion. The mother began climbing Rapunzel's hair when Rapunzel got some scissors and cut her hair. Her mother fell to her death.

Annabelle Staddon (12)

Plympton Academy, Plympton

RAPUNZEL'S BIG MISTAKE

I found myself lying, staring and wondering why I didn't fit in. I wanted to. I wanted to find some reassurance so I looked through some old photos but there weren't any of me at all!

I decided to go to town, even though I was not allowed. It was scary but I was excited the first time I saw the lights. It was amazing. Then I saw a man, he started chasing me. I screamed and ran but he got me. I was found dead.

Emily Bennett (13)
Plympton Academy, Plympton

HANSEL AND GRETEL, BUT...

It was a normal day until me and Hansel went into the deep forest. We were foraging and we saw a house, a gingerbread house, so we went inside because we were hungry. There was an old lady in there. She greeted us and sat us down and fed us, but she took Hansel by the wrist and killed him, cooked him and ate him! I was horrified! I ran into the forest with blood on my face. I ran and ran and then a wolf pounced...

Jack Simpson (12)
Plympton Academy, Plympton

THE TALE OF GOLDILOCKS, THE GIRL WHO HAD A WORLD OF HER OWN

It was a normal day until I heard an ear-bleeding scream coming from downstairs. Tripping over my two left feet, I ran down the stairs to find my cousin, Goldilocks, lying hopelessly on the floor with three bowls smashed into millions of pieces. As I fell to my knees to help pick up the bowls, my uncle picked me up with his bear-like hands and threw me across the room...

Jessica Richmond (13)
Plympton Academy, Plympton

THE TEAM KILLER

The Hobbit was on a trek to find one of his masters. He was sent with a team, his team was the worst he could have asked for. He thought of a plan to kill them off one by one so no one would notice. So he started to kill them. First, he killed Frodo, then he killed Luke, the Nori. He disfigured them and buried them in the ground.

Nathan Annetts (13)

Plympton Academy, Plympton

SHREK'S FAMILY NIGHTMARE

Shrek came back from his wedding to Fiona. He was quite tired, so he went to sleep. When he was in a deep sleep, he had a dream about having a ton of children. In the dream he said, "What's that noise?" Fiona was shouting for Shrek to help. He ran in saying, "What? What is wrong?"
"I need help with the babies!" Fiona replied.
"What ba-" asked Shrek, then he saw the babies and collapsed.
He woke up to Donkey shouting, "Shrek!"
Shrek said, "I just had the worst dream..."
Donkey said, "There's a situation."
Shrek saw the babies...

Holly Hesler (13)
Wellfield Community School, Wingate

A CAPTURE GONE WRONG

Once, there was a girl named Belle. She lived with her father, an ingenious inventor.

One day, Belle was captured by a hideous beast! Belle kept having arguments with the beast.

"Shut up!" shouted Belle.

"How about you do!" screeched the beast.

At this, Belle ran to the kitchen and grabbed a sharpened knife. "Argh!" screamed the beast, as he fell to the floor bleeding.

Belle ran out of the ominous castle she had been captive in for so long.

Covered in blood, the young murderer went home to her father. She never thought about the poor beast ever again!

Efa Hope Wilson (12)

Wellfield Community School, Wingate

RAPUNZEL: THE TWISTED TALE

Birds beyond the impenetrable walls awoke Rapunzel. Endless days consisted of her stepmother holding her hostage, dreaming of a way to escape. Her hair was the solution. She tossed golden locks out of the castle window. Sliding down her hair, she touched the vibrant grass for the first time. Seeing a figure take shelter behind a tree, the peaceful moment evaporated.

Rapunzel slept, her soft breaths echoing. The familiar figure emerged from her cupboard, reaching for the knife on their belt. The figure escaped the tower soon after, leaving a bloody trail behind. They were later identified as Flynn Rider.

Layla Richards (12)
Wellfield Community School, Wingate

RAPUNZEL'S ESCAPE GOES WRONG

There once was a young princess who was stolen. Mother Gothel was the thief of the child (Rapunzel) but Rapunzel didn't know it. She had always been locked inside her castle because her 'mother' didn't want her to leave.

A few years later, she suddenly became more curious about what the outdoors was like. Over time, she got too bored and left.

This is amazing, thought Rapunzel.

Suddenly, Rapunzel turned to find Mother Gothel! This was the moment her 'mother' reached her breaking point.

From that day, Rapunzel was never seen outside the castle ever again.

Katie Colling (11)
Wellfield Community School, Wingate

CINDERELLA

Cinderella was a prisoner in her own home. She was hopeless until one night she encountered a mysterious figure claiming to be her fairy godmother. She granted her beautiful clothes and instructed her to go to the prince's ball. But only until midnight for it would all wear off.
All was going well - the prince loved her, she could be saved. But at midnight she left and the prince didn't know who she was. Suddenly, her slipper fell off her foot, which could've identified her, but it broke and so Cinderella would continue to live in prison, completely distraught.

Dexter Basford (12)
Wellfield Community School, Wingate

THE WHITE SNAKE

There once was a king who knew every piece of information in the kingdom. No one knew how, but many rumours spread across the land. Every dinner time after everyone had left, the king was brought another plate. Even the servants didn't know what was under the cover. The king slowly took off the cover and a small white snake slithered out and hissed all of the events in the kingdom that day into the king's ear.

One day, the snake wasn't there. The king no longer knew information others need to know. The people called him a fraud.

Ruby Allen (12)
Wellfield Community School, Wingate

HIGHER POWER!

All was quiet in the house until Alia opened the door. She saw the biggest group of people ever. They were her parents' friends so they were very big tyrants - very rude and villainous. She saw piles and piles of money being exchanged. Rushing through the doors, Alia insisted to stop this gang at once. Everyone glared at Alia and laughed, taking steps as slow as a tortoise's towards her. The scary and repulsive gang picked up their bats as Alia screamed and ran to find help, but no one could save her now! She was never seen again!

Eve Bateman (12)
Wellfield Community School, Wingate

JACK'S DISAPPEARANCE

Jack woke up with a list of jobs. First, it said: 'Go and buy a cow'. He took some money and went to the market. On the way there a brittle old lady stopped him to ask, "Would you like to buy these magic beans?"

He took some home and showed his mother. She was outraged, Jack was ordered to get all the money back. Whilst at the end of the market street, he stumbled upon an abandoned field. After walking miles, he stumbled upon a rustic building. He entered it and was never ever heard of again!

Nicole Luke (12)
Wellfield Community School, Wingate

SHREK GONE ROGUE

Shrek was a menacing evil ogre, with a donkey as a sidekick. The ogre lived in a shack outside the forest and on the other side of his house was a swamp. He walked around mocking and scaring people, and even sometimes he would attack poor innocent people. He often had battles with the local superheroes and got beaten every time.

Shrek went to rob a bank, but he got caught so he launched Donkey and then started to battle. He got the upper hand and for the first time, he defeated the heroes and lived life grumpily.

Aiden Ridley (11)
Wellfield Community School, Wingate

THE SECRETS OF LITTLE RED RIDING HOOD

It was sunset when Red reached her grandma's. She was sat knitting on her armchair when she opened the door. A quiet squeal escaped her lips when she saw Red. "What are you doing here?" her grandma asked. "You need to leave before the moon rises!"
But it was too late. The full moon rose above them. That's when Red started to change, her eyes shone bright yellow, her feet turned to paws... and stood before her grandma was a wolf. It jumped towards her, showing sharp yellow teeth...

Amy Reeve (12)
Wellfield Community School, Wingate

HUMPTY-DUMPTY HAD A GREAT FALL!

Humpty-Dumpty was an egg. Although he was an egg, Humpty loved to climb, he was due to hatch in a few days. One day Humpty went to the local park and climbed up onto the wall. He sat on it for a good 20 minutes, enjoying the peaceful breeze of the wind and the stunning nature around him. Humpty looked down to see how high up he was. Humpty-Dumpty leaned too far over and fell off at a high speed, but... he landed on his feet! Humpty hatched into a cat! Humpty enjoyed the rest of his life climbing.

Frankie Garraghan (12)
Wellfield Community School, Wingate

ONE SMALL MISTAKE

I always knew my mother wanted the best for me. Though, one small mistake wasn't going to hurt anyone, apart from him. He'd promised to love me forever, yet he had run off with a superior girl.

A dark night came overhead; it was perfect. I trudged towards him and forcefully pulled my arm up and vigorously brought it down, the bat alongside me. It swung across, knocking him out. I felt powerful, like a god.

I arrived home to my resentful mother. "Where have you been?" she asked.

Grinning venomously, I replied, "All in a day's work."

Grace Mitchell (13)
Westfield Academy, Yeovil

YoungWriters Est. 1991

YOUNG WRITERS INFORMATION

We hope you have enjoyed reading this book – and that you will continue to in the coming years.

If you're a young writer who enjoys reading and creative writing, or the parent of an enthusiastic poet or story writer, do visit our website **www.youngwriters.co.uk**. Here you will find free competitions, workshops and games, as well as recommended reads, a poetry glossary and our blog. There's lots to keep budding writers motivated to write!

If you would like to order further copies of this book, or any of our other titles, then please give us a call or order via your online account.

Young Writers
Remus House
Coltsfoot Drive
Peterborough
PE2 9BF
(01733) 890066
info@youngwriters.co.uk

Join in the conversation!
Tips, news, giveaways and much more!

 YoungWritersUK  YoungWritersCW 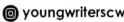 youngwriterscw